Holiday HAVOC

RECKLESS BASTARDS MC
MAYHEM, NV

WALL STREET JOURNAL & USA TODAY BESTSELLING AUTHOR
KB WINTERS

Copyright and Disclaimer

This book is a work of fiction. The names, characters, places and incidents are products of the writer's imagination and have been used fictitiously and are not to be construed as real. Any resemblance to persons, living or dead, actual events, locales or organizations is entirely coincidental.

Copyright © 2018 Book Boyfriends Publishing

All rights reserved. No part of this publication may be reproduced, stored in or introduced into a retrieval system, or transmitted, in any form, or by any means (electronic, mechanical, photocopying, recording, or otherwise) without the prior written permission of the copyright owner. The author acknowledges the trademarked status and trademark owners of various products referenced in this work of fiction, which have been used without permission. The publication/use of the trademarks is not authorized, associated with, or sponsored by the trademark owners.

Table of Contents

Copyright and Disclaimer ii
Prologue - Stitch 7
Chapter One - Cross.. 15
Chapter Two - Stitch 21
Chapter Three - Lasso... 29
Chapter Four - Max...35
Chapter Five - Gunnar 45
Chapter Six - Jag...55
Chapter Seven - Stitch 61
Chapter Eight - Gunnar 69
Chapter Nine - Cross... 83
Chapter Ten - Jag... 95
Chapter Eleven - Gunnar 111
Chapter Twelve – Golden Boy 121
Chapter Thirteen - Stitch 131
Chapter Fourteen - Jag 149
Chapter Fifteen – Cross 163
Chapter Sixteen - Stitch 175
Chapter Seventeen - Max...................................193
Chapter Eighteen - Cross 205

Chapter Nineteen - Gunnar...............................215
Chapter Twenty - Savior....................................229
Chapter Twenty-One - Lasso...........................241
Chapter Twenty-Two - Stitch...........................249
Chapter Twenty-Three - Max...........................257
Chapter Twenty-Four - Gunnar.......................265
Chapter Twenty-Five - Stitch...........................277
Chapter Twenty-Six - Golden Boy..................285
Chapter Twenty-Seven - Gunnar....................293
Chapter Twenty-Eight – Cross........................305
Chapter Twenty-Nine - Jag..............................319
Chapter Thirty - Stitch......................................333
Chapter Thirty-One - Max................................339
Chapter Thirty-Two - Jag..................................345
Chapter Thirty-Three-Cross.............................355
Chapter Thirty-Four - Stitch............................371
Epilogue - Max..381

Holiday Havoc

Reckless Bastards MC

By Wall Street Journal & USA Today Bestselling Author

KB Winters

Prologue - Stitch

"Damn woman, you trying to wear me out?" Marisol was a woman made for a good hard fuck. Just over five feet with big double D tits, a tiny waist and the kind of ass a man could hold on to while he rammed her from behind. She made my regular trips to the Reno area worth the long ride on my bike.

Her deep laugh was husky with a touch of smoke and even though my cock was still wet with her juices, she was ready for more. "I'm not trying. Not yet anyway."

She turned to face me and slid her hand down my chest, nails scraping along the way, doing her best to get my cock as hard as a steel rod. She dipped her head and licked a trail of heat from my nipples straight to my dick. "Part of you is ready."

That little purr did it to me or maybe it was those thick lips that wrapped around me and slid up and down. Hot and wet, she took all of me. Deep. Again and again she ate my cock like it was the only thing she needed to survive. I closed my eyes, hips flexing as she sucked me like a pro. "Fuck, yeah." I could barely get the words out when she swallowed around the tip of my cock. The girl knew how to treat a dick and that was only my second favorite thing about her.

Being with Marisol was easy because she didn't expect more than a good time and a great fuck when I was able to make it up here. But damn my cock missed her when I had to go back home to Mayhem. Especially when she took me deep as my cock hardened and swelled, swallowing every drop when I shot my load down her throat. She pulled back with a grin, licking her lips. "Someone's been listening to me?"

"Hey, if a chick tells me to drink more fruit juice because it makes my jizz taste sweeter, I'll fucking drink a gallon of that shit every day. The way you give head, I'd live on that shit if you asked me to."

She laughed again and collapsed onto the bed beside me, one hand resting on my thigh and that was the only physical connection between us. Marisol wasn't a sentimental woman. She didn't cuddle and she never gave me sweet kisses when I left, only kisses so fiery I had to have her one final time before I said goodbye. "I'll keep that in mind."

We both fell silent and that was another thing I liked about Marisol. She didn't feel the need to fill every silence with words. With questions about feelings and all the shit that only complicated things. No, she was cool as hell and so chill that I found myself wanting to see her more and more.

Too bad she had secrets of her own.

"So when are you gonna come visit me in Mayhem?"

She sighed that disappointed sigh that I swore women took a class to perfect. "I would love to but my boss is kind of a dick."

That didn't sound right, in fact, it sounded like an excuse. "If you don't want to come, just say so. My feelings won't get hurt, darlin'."

"I do want to but things are..." she trailed off in search of a word but I already knew what it was. Exactly what I went out of my way to avoid.

"Complicated?"

"Yeah." She sighed again and propped her head up in her hand, long dark brown hair cascading all around her shoulders, making her honey brown skin look damn near white by contrast. "I started working as a bookkeeper when I was in school getting a degree in accounting."

"You're a college girl?" I teased because the news was, well news to me. We'd only met about two months ago and had seen each other a handful of times . We knew more about each other's bodies than we did about our respective lives. "I should have known with your vocabulary."

"It's called reading, Stitch. Try it some time." Those full lips pulled up into a sultry grin that made me want to take her again. Right now, though, my cock was still spent.

"Hey, I read," I retorted.

"What Bikers and Babes or something?"

"Yeah, it has really great articles or haven't you heard?" I replied.

She smiled but it wasn't her usual. "Okay," I said reluctantly. "Tell me what's wrong." Fuck. I hoped it wasn't feelings.

"Well, I work for a grow operation that expanded as soon as states started legalizing pot. My boss is…not your average boss, let's just say that for now. So I started working there a few years ago and…well, I haven't been able to leave. Yet."

"That sounds ominous as fuck, Marisol."

She huffed out a bitter laugh that said more than her words ever could. "Try living it. Anyway, I'd love to get the fuck out of Reno for a while. I really would. But I can't."

I heard her loud and clear. "You're fucking your boss." It wasn't a question or a judgment. She was free to do whatever she pleased and she didn't owe me any explanations.

"Yes and no. When I met him, I thought he was just this amazing older guy who had his shit together. I mean he had a business and he seemed to be really interested in me. Not my body, just me." She blew out a long breath and dropped her forehead on my chest. "I didn't find out until a year of seeing him and doing his books that he was married. Fucking married. With children. Bastard turned *me* into the other woman." She was still pissed about it, which made me suspicious.

"But you were already in love with him?"

She barked out a laugh. "Fuck no. I wanted to leave and get the fuck outta Dodge."

"But?" Jesus Christ, women could drag a five minute story and turn it into a goddamned odyssey.

"But," she sighed as if the weight of the world rested on her shoulders, "it wasn't quite that easy because in two years of dating I had no fucking clue who I was dating."

"And who *were* you dating?"

"A bad guy. A really fucking bad guy."

"Just a bad guy? Nothing else?"

"Yes, he is a really, really bad guy." She didn't say any more about him and I didn't push it. Honestly, the club had enough fucking trouble because of our women and I didn't want to add to it. Not while I was still trying to find my place as a full patch Reckless Bastard. "So yeah, Stitch, I'd love to go visit you. See your town and spend some unsupervised time in Vegas, but I can't."

Which meant she was involved with someone serious and seriously fucked in the head. And if I kept fucking around with her, I might land my club in more shit and that was the last fucking thing we needed. I needed to find out who this dickhead was.

"Well when you can, let me know." She smiled when I leaned in to kiss her, my cock already growing harder by the second. When she moved against me, I slipped inside her tight, wet pussy and gave her a good hard fuck. One that would have to last me until I made it back up to Reno again.

HOLIDAY HAVOC

Chapter One - Cross

"Do we have any new club business?" It was strange as fuck to sit in the Merry Mayhem room and talk about mundane shit. For the past few months, hell for the past few years, the Reckless Bastards have been through one shitstorm after another. Gangsters, politicians, bikers and even fucking crooked cops had tried to fuck us from all sides and every fucking time we came out on top.

It felt good. Damn good.

"Yeah, I do." Golden Boy, who'd recently chopped a few inches off his signature blonde ponytail, stood with a reluctant grin. "Me and Lasso need the next week free of the club rotation." To make sure all of our businesses were covered, we all took turns tending to shared club interests.

"Why?" Not that I would say no. I treated my men like family because that was what we were.

"Don't you know, Prez?" Lasso stood, wearing his patented shit-eating grin as he slapped Golden Boy on the back. Hard. Golden Boy sent an elbow flying right to his gut, making him grunt. "GB and I are heading to the City of Angels for a tattoo expo and competition. First prize is fifty grand plus a feature on Tat Magazine. Pretty fuckin' cool, yeah?"

"Hell yeah!" Though we didn't always go in for high profile events like this. After the shit hit the fan with a crooked Governor, the CIA and a crooked fucking councilman, the Reckless Bastards weren't exactly keeping a low profile. Plus, fifty grand was a nice payday. "We need some drinks."

Stitch stood with a smile and opened the door. "Any Bitches out there? 'Cause we need drinks and plenty of 'em!"

"Yeah, Stitch, you're a real asset to the club," Savior joked, sparking up a joint with a relaxed grin.

"You're welcome, grandpa." Stitch loved to give everyone shit and he was good at it. He was also young as hell and determined to prove himself. "Should we add some prune juice to your beer?"

"Nah, I prefer lime, shithead." Savior laughed and passed the joint, blowing out a large plume of smoke. "So. Mandy's pregnant. Just a few weeks." The room fell silent, everyone shocked because she'd been so focused on her career, making high profile confections for high rollers who flocked to the Siren Casino & Resort just to see her magical chocolate creations. And Savior, well the man was solid and reliable. But he was about as paternal as a fucking brick wall. "Say something, fuckers!"

Max and Lasso were on their feet first, smacking his back too hard with wide smiles and words of congratulations. "It's about damn time," Lasso said with another clap to the back. "I was starting to think your jizz had turned to dust."

"Asshole," Savior grumbled, but there was no hiding the happiness on his face. "I'm happy, but fuck, what the fuck do I know about being a dad?"

"The same that any of us knows," Max assured him. "It's like riding a bike. The books only tell you so much and the only way to figure out how not to crash your bike is to crash it a couple dozen times."

"Yeah, thanks. Hope my kid survives the crash known as me." His sarcastic tone only sent up another round of laughter and congratulations. "Anyway, that's my news."

A knock sounded at the door before it opened and three prospects brought in the booze. The Reckless Bitches were completely barred from the Merry Mayhem room. The new prospects could enter when invited.

"We got beers and we got booze." The threesome was led by Black, a twenty-three year old prospect with a short black buzz cut and eyes so dark they might as well be black. He was a damn cool customer but a former sharpshooter who'd been dishonorably discharged when he beat the fuck out of his commanding officer for taking advantage of a fellow solider.

"Thanks. Stay and have a drink." That shocked the shit out of all three of the prospects because we had put them through the ringer this past year. But with all the shit the club had been through, we needed new blood. Tough new blood at that.

"What are we drinking to?" The question came from Lex, another prospect with bright red hair and so many freckles it was hard to believe he'd spent almost a decade doing wet work for Uncle Sam.

Stich barked, "Savior found enough jizz in his nuts to knock up Mandy!"

Savior grunted, "Asshole," at Stitch and snatched the joint from his mouth, handing it to Lex.

"Congratulations, man." Black lifted his beer, smiling to himself when Savior glared at him.

"Yeah, thanks. All of you Bastards."

Lasso pounded on the table, his favorite way to get everyone excited. Hyped up. One by one everyone joined in, pounding in a staccato beat as they chanted. "Mayhem! Mayhem! Mayhem!" On and on it went until the room was a roar of noise and pounding fists on solid wood and metal.

Goddamn it felt good to have life back to normal.

Chapter Two - Stitch

"Oh come on, man! Why not?" Letting out a long breath, I followed Cross out of his office at the clubhouse to one of the picnic tables we kept out back. "This could be a win-win for the club."

My Prez sighed the way he always did when he didn't want to talk about something. Or make a fucking decision. "Because I don't know these people and I don't like to do business with strangers."

I wanted to point out that he had no fucking problem working with the Sons of Sin when it suited him, but all of this shit was his decision. "So, meet Reed and he won't be a damn stranger, man! Listen, he used to be a scientist for the government, and he helped them make huge strides in their medical marijuana program."

"Yeah? Then why isn't he there now?"

I clenched my jaws to avoid the smartass comment that was on the tip of my tongue. "Because he figured he could use his considerable skills to make a shit ton of money when states started legalizing weed. You know you can't fucking retire on a government pension."

"I'll think about it, Stitch."

"Bullshit. I know I'm the new guy around here but just tell me to fuck off if you don't want a crack at this. Reed's shit is good, damn good and high potency. Plus, he does all that funky shit with terpenes and oils, you know the stuff that rich stoners pay a premium for." His operation was a thing of beauty and the reason I'd been making regular trips up to the Reno area.

"So you want me to ignore our current grower? We have a solid relationship with them." Cross was stretching now but I had to give it one final shot. This would show him, hell it would show the whole club that I wasn't just some fucked up new patch out to have a good time.

"No, not ignore them. But what if the fields get torched again? Or stolen? Or a fuckin' DEA raid? Then we'll be shit outta luck for at least a few months. Come on. Check out Reed's operation, try a few strains and get some of that new stuff that'll bring more tourists and high rollers into the dispensaries." Why in the hell was this so hard to get? I knew he was trying to keep things even after all the shit we'd been through, but he was also being a pussy. "Just meet Reed and see his op." If he met Reed and they didn't gel, I'd give it a rest.

"Moon is going out of town this week to visit a couple recluse artists so I'm on daddy duty. I can't spend a whole day out of Mayhem." A smile lit up his face when he talked about his woman and her little boy. The kid was too damn smart and so talkative it was hard not to like him, especially since he seemed to breathe new life into Cross. The club was the better for it, but now our Prez was playing it safe. Too safe. "I can't do it but I appreciate your initiative, Stitch."

My shoulders fell at his tone. It was a tone I knew well. "Right. See you around, man." I guess I was going back to being a background player.

"Take Gunnar with you."

I froze and turned as a slow smile formed on my face. "You won't regret this." I dug into my pocket and pulled out a tall purple pill bottle. "Try it out." I tossed the bottle to him and he caught it with a knowing smile.

"You're one relentless motherfucker, Stitch."

"Thanks, Prez. I'll go find Grumpy Gunnar." The sound of Cross' laughter echoed behind me as I went through the front entrance of the clubhouse in search of Gunnar. I found him playing with his baby sister Maisie, lifting her chubby little body in the air while she giggled and kicked her legs.

"What do you want, Stitch?"

Gunnar was such a fucking grumpy bastard that it was too fun to screw with him so I plucked Maisie from his hands which only made her laugh and kick more. "You like me best, don'tcha sweetheart?" I looked down at Gunnar's dark scowl and laughed when she planted a sopping wet kiss on my nose. "See, it's all the ladies."

"What the fuck do you want?"

I told him all about Reed and my next trip. "Cross said to take you with me. Take a look around and give him your impressions. End of week work for you?"

"No, Stitch, it doesn't. I can't just leave Maisie for a whole fucking day. I have to find a sitter so I'll let you know."

Which meant he would wait me out and try to get out of it. "Figure it out and come find me. Maisie and I will be out in the play area."

"Asshole," he growled behind me but I just laughed and carried the laughing two year old to the swings we'd put out back when it became clear the wives, girlfriends and kids would be hanging around the clubhouse a lot more.

While I pushed Maisie on the swing my thoughts went to Marisol. She'd been acting strange for the past few months. On edge but claiming she wasn't; terrified but calling it stress. She'd lost weight and she wasn't sleeping, and apparently she didn't want my fucking help. But for some reason that was exactly what I wanted to do, help her out of whatever trouble she found herself in right now. Since it was just me and Maisie outside, I decided to give her a call. A couple weeks had passed since I'd been up there and I was due for a trip. With or without Gunnar.

"Hey you," she said in that husky voice that would have made my dick hard if I wasn't pushing an infant on a swing. "Now isn't a good time. Do you mind if I call you back?"

"Who the fuck is that? Quien es?" It was a man's voice, high pitched with a thick Spanish accent.

"None of your business," she grunted through clenched teeth. "Look," she said, talking to me again. "I have to deal with this right now but I'll call you back."

"No you won't! Tell that pendejo to fuck off!"

"Is that him, the married fucker?"

"Yes," she sighed, sounding exhausted and resigned to her fate.

"Want me to come up there?"

"Not now," she whispered. "He's jealous and angry. I can handle it."

Of course she could. She'd been raised by an alcoholic father who'd only gotten worse when her mother died. "That's not the point. You shouldn't have to handle that asshole by yourself. What's his name?"

"Never mind. I have to call you back." Then she ended the fucking call and it took everything within me not to hop on my bike and go knock that fucker out.

But Marisol didn't *want* my help. No, she wanted to handle this by herself. And I didn't like it one bit.

Chapter Three - Lasso

"Just be careful. Something feels weird and I don't know what." Rocky had her beautiful body pressed up against mine, arms wrapped tight around me, big green eyes filled with worry.

"Aw, sugar, you worried about me?" As much as I hated to admit it, my daddy was right. There *was* nothing in this world like the love of a good woman. And Rocky was a damn good woman. She was *my* woman. "Don't be babe, I've got two damn good reasons to come back. And I will. Always."

Her mouth tipped into a soft, lopsided grin. "I know that, cowboy. I'm just telling you to be careful."

It was sweet that she always worried about me and considering all the shit that had fallen on the club the past few years, I couldn't blame her. Instead I kissed her, long and slow, hard as I pushed her body against the fridge until she moaned. "I'll be fine and careful, Rocky. What I need you to do is rest up because when I get back I'm gonna put another baby in you."

A loud throaty laugh bubbled out of her and she smacked my arm. "Why don't you worry about winning the big prize first?"

"Like there's any doubt who's taking the cash and the trophy home." Since the tattoo shop wasn't a club business, Golden Boy and I would split the fifty grand cash prize, which only made me want to win even more. "Jag's gonna stop by to check on you and Dallas while I'm gone."

Her smile lit up again but those green eyes nearly cut a hole through me. "That's not necessary. Between baby yoga, finger painting and creating Halloween costumes for all the kids, I'll be plenty busy. And I'm sure Jag has better things to do."

I wished that was true but he hadn't been himself since his girl, Vivi, disappeared to the east coast with the CIA. "Better than playing with his godson? Un-fucking-likely." He loved my boy as much as I did and I knew he'd make sure they were protected in my absence. "Don't forget the sexy Halloween costume you promised me."

She laughed. "Oh I won't. I've got your measurements and everything."

I frowned. "Wait, that wasn't the agreement. *You're* supposed to have the sexy costume."

One hand pressed against my chest and Rocky took a step back. "No, you said, 'make something sexy for me for Halloween' and I did."

"You little minx."

She giggled, fucking giggled and all the blood in my body made a short trip to my cock. "Damn right. Besides, every good cowboy needs a horse."

"A horse?"

"Yep. Dallas is going to be a cowboy." Her smile was filled with mischief. "I've never ridden a horse before."

"Damn I love you, Rocky." She laughed as my mouth scraped against her neck, her throat and across her collarbone. She was as delicate as she was tough and it was a combination I couldn't resist.

"That's good cowboy, because I love you too."

It never got old to hear and it never failed to get my blood good and hot, and thick like molasses. "Is Baby Dallas still sleeping?"

"For another half hour. At least." Her voice was already breathy, thick with desire as her arms tightened around me. Pulled me close so her lips could devour me, so her tongue could taste every inch of my mouth while my hands slid down her back and under her robe. One hand squeezing ass cheeks so round from having my baby while the other slipped inside the opening of her robe and between the folds of her pussy. Hot and slick. For me. "Don't make me wait, cowboy."

Did I mention that I loved it when she called me cowboy? Two fingers slid into her slick pussy, deep and she let out a low moan that had me ready to take her, hard and fast in the kitchen. But my cock wouldn't come out until she had at least one orgasm—maybe two—because nothing felt better than sliding in to a dripping and pulsing pussy. When that first orgasm poured from her, I was wild like an animal, shoving down my sweatpants and lifting her before impaling her on my hard cock. "Oh fuck, Rocky. You're so fucking wet."

"That's all you, big guy." She smiled and licked a trail of wet heat up my neck while I held her, thrusting deep. "I'm going to miss this while you're gone."

I thrust deeper and harder, using my body to keep her where I wanted her, fucking her so hard, she'd miss me every damn second I was away from her. She cried out and clenched around me, letting out that little half-grunt, half-sigh that always accompanied her orgasms. With Rocky limp in my arms, I held her and pounded my way to orgasm, skin tingling at the way she scraped her teeth along my skin. "Oh fuck, Rocky babe!"

She laughed and dropped her head on my shoulder, tightening her legs around my waist. "Good job, cowboy. That'll tide me over until you come back." She kissed me again and slid down my body before tightening her robe and stepping away. "Go say goodbye to your son before you leave."

I wasn't ready to leave, hell I hadn't spent more than a day or two away since Dallas was born and I wasn't sure I could do it.

But I would. For my family, I'd do anything.

Chapter Four - Max

"I don't know why in the hell Golden Boy asked me to show up this week, it's not like you can't handle this on your own." I didn't mind spending a few days at Get Ink'd but I knew jack shit about drawing up tattoos. I only painted for therapy and I only kept it up because I loved to paint with my woman. At least when we found time between taking care of our kids.

"Because someone, *me*, needs to do ink and piercings while someone else, *you*, takes calls and mans the register." Jag grinned over at me with a smartass smirk. "Besides, the artists coming in this week can handle a few extra slabs of skin while you oversee the important stuff." Golden Boy had connected with two big name tattoo artists looking to spend some time in Vegas and grow their brand. He had some notion it would help the club but I didn't see how.

"The ink isn't important?"

"Yeah, but money is too. And we have the ink part handled. If you really don't wanna be here," he began and trailed off in that reasonable way that was damn annoying when it was aimed at you. "With The Inky Minx and Indigo coming in, we'll have more than enough ink to worry about."

"Okay, fine. If you want to me here to hold your hand, Jag, I'm happy to help out."

"Dick," he smirked and went to set up his work station before his first appointment showed up.

Every time I set foot inside the shop, it amazed me that my brother was able to create this beautiful shop from the worst shit that had ever happened to him. I'd barely survived PTSD but he'd been wrongfully convicted for six years and had somehow found a way to make it into something good. I was damn proud of him and I knew our mom would've been proud as well, if she was still around. "We're not open yet," I called out from behind the counter where I was unloading after-care kits.

"Your wife told me I could find you here." I knew that voice. I'd heard it too many times over the past few years.

"Dodds." I stood to my full height. "What are you doing here?" I couldn't hate on the guy because he'd not only saved Moon's life but he was also instrumental in bringing down most of Roadkill MC and the crooked politician working with them. "Came to get a thin blue line tat?"

His lips twitched with amusement as he walked in, looking around in that intrusive way of law enforcement all over the world. "Maybe another time. I have a question or two. For you."

My body tensed right away. Not because I thought we were in trouble, hell the club had finally rebounded from all the shit thrown at us last year, but cops asking questions was rarely a good thing. "Do I need my lawyer?"

He shook his head and leaned against the counter, looking more relaxed than I'd ever seen him. "Nope. I have questions that you might not like but I need answers." His brown eyes were clear and sober. Serious as hell.

"Ask." I might not answer them but I knew the club as a whole owed him so I squared my shoulders and looked him straight on. And waited.

"Are the Reckless Bastards doin' business with cartels now?"

"What? Fuck no!" We had a hard and fast rule as a club that the cartels were off limits. They were always into bad shit like trafficking kids and selling arms indiscriminately. We were no angels but we had our limits. "Why would you ask that?"

Dodds sighed, the weight of his new job weighing heavy on his shoulders. It couldn't have been easy going from Internal Affairs and taking down a well-respected but dirty as fuck cop, to being a top detective for the Gangs & Drugs task force. "We've spotted a few known cartel members over at Siren Casino & Resort when their tats popped up on surveillance. I'm just trying to figure out if they're here to experience 'What happens in Vegas' or if they're here to do business."

"Shit." Cartel visits were no good for anyone. Even if they were here for fun, they were notorious for trying to squeeze other business out if they saw an opening. "Reckless Bastards don't fuck with cartels but I'll talk to Cross and see if he's heard anything."

"Sounds good. I didn't want to ask these questions with the kid around," he said, referring to Beau who was Cross's number one fan. "Any intel you have would be appreciated and anonymous."

"Appreciate it. Don't forget to come back for that tat, Detective."

He laughed again and gave a quick wave before heading out of the shop just as a guy with almost clear blue eyes showed up and stared at me. "I'm Indigo."

I nodded and motioned to the big room Lasso usually occupied since this guy was known for sleeves and big ass tats. For the next couple hours I sat up front listening to music and answering the most idiotic fucking questions from potential customers. They were all tourists and didn't have a clue about tattoos. "You'll have to come into the shop to get that answer," became my mantra to callers by the time lunch rolled around. "Jesus, fuck! You have got to be kidding me."

"Callers getting' to ya, Max?"

I growled at Jag who looked far too fucking happy for a guy who'd been hunched over a sweaty hog-riding weekend warrior for the past three hours. "There should be a fucking IQ test before you get inked."

He laughed, shrugging it off like the calm and collected guy he was. "Ink is serious business for most people." He waited a beat and then another, until Indigo stepped out for a smoke. "So, Dodds?"

I gave him a quick rundown of what the detective wanted and he let out a long, low whistle. "He didn't say which cartel though?"

"If any tattoos popped up on surveillance, I can find them when I get home." The guy was a damn genius when it came to working on computers and techy shit and sometimes, I wondered why the hell he'd become a Reckless Bastard in the first place.

"You can find what came up on surveillance?"

Jag snorted. "Who the fuck you talking to man?"

"Okay, okay. Sorry. I told him I'd talk to Cross to see if he knew anything but there wasn't much else to say." We both sat there in momentary silence, probably thinking the same damn thing. *Please don't let more shit be headed to Mayhem.* "Any word on Vivi?" It was Jag's least favorite conversation these days but the guy needed to talk about it. At least according to my wife.

"No," he snarled. "She keeps saying she'll be back soon but *soon* isn't a goddamn date, is it? You think she changed her mind?"

Normally I would give Jag shit and tell him she probably *had* changed her mind but if the CIA had scooped Jana up from me, I'd be burning down every bridge to drag her back. "No man, I don't. I think the feds will squeeze every fucking second out of her they legally can. You just have to be patient. Vivi doesn't seem like the kind of girl to lie about her feelings. Right?"

"Riiight," he sighed reluctantly. "She's a woman. They change their mind. Daily." Vivi was tough as nails with steel running through her spine, and just as smart as Jag.

"Maybe try focusing on something other than Vivi. Get your house ready for when she does come back and add some freaky computer love shit for you nerds." He flipped me off like I expected and we both laughed.

"Jana has turned you into a pussy," he accused and that pulled a bigger laugh from me. "All romantic and in love."

"Well, romance is hard to come by with two kiddos in the house, but with a little creativity we make it work."

"No shit, when is the next one coming?"

The thought of another kid made me smile. Charlie and Jameson were a handful and I loved the hell out of them but a little girl with her mama's hair and eyes, well that sounded like my version of heaven. "Well, we are constantly practicing."

"Not interested in the deets, man."

I smiled with a hint of mischief. "I mean I have learned plenty of tricks—"

"Jana is like a sister to me, man. Stopppp."

"My favorite is to drive her wild. Quietly." I wiggled my thick fingers in the air.

Jag pushed off the counter and took a step back. "Better go get ready for my next client."

"Don't be a pussy, Jag."

He shot me a grin. "I'll just wait until she tells me all the details and fuck with you later."

I snorted a little. Maybe working at GET INK'D for the next few days wouldn't be so bad after all.

Chapter Five - Gunnar

The last fucking thing I wanted was to take this Goddamn road trip with Stitch, but the fucking kid was relentless. He'd badgered Cross until he gave in, sending me on a half day's ride up to Reno. Fucking Reno. Instead of hanging out with Maisie, who was growing faster than a weed. She was with Rocky while my ass was numb four hours into the trip. "What's wrong with our current supplier?"

Stitch grinned. "Nothing except we're fucked if something happens to them. Plus I know Reed and his shit is good. Real good."

I believed that. The kid wasn't just a regular social pot smoker, no, he was a certified fucking stoner. "Yeah, all right. But could this dude live fucking closer than bum-fuck Egypt?"

The kid flashed another smile around his bacon chili cheeseburger at some roadside burger joint where we stopped to refuel before we made it to this guy

Reed's operation. "He could but wait until you see it, then you can talk shit."

Christ, was I ever that fucking young and naive? "You know you're a brother even if this doesn't pan out?"

He nodded while he finished chewing and shoved a handful of fries in his mouth. "I know but this is a good move because right now most of Reed's stuff goes to Cali, which means people will come to us for the really good shit." He stood and tossed his trash, returning with two bottles of water. "You don't have to be such a grumpy asshole about it, you know. I know you think I'm just a fuckin' kid and I don't know shit but give this a chance."

Well fuck, now he went and made me feel bad. And I knew I had to give him what he was asking for because he was right. I was being an asshole and the kid just wanted to matter. Plus raising Maisie cost a lot of fucking money and if he was right, it would mean a bigger payday for all of us. "Fine but I'll be honest."

Like the kid he was at only twenty-six, Stitch smiled a smile of someone with something to prove. "I expect nothing less. When was the last time you were nice enough to spare someone's fucking feelings?"

I may have been a hard bastard but I wanted to give Maisie more than our mom ever gave me and definitely more than the six weeks she'd spent with Maisie before she was put into the ground. Maisie deserved better, hell probably more than I could ever give her, but I wanted her to have everything. And better weed meant bigger profits, which spelled a better, normal life for my sister. "Come on, let's get outta here before my ass remembers what it's like to have feeling."

Stitch kicked a leg over his bike and grinned. "None of us will respect you less if you get one of those old man ass cushions."

"Asshole!"

He laughed and flipped me off, revving the engine as he sped off. Yeah, I smiled as I caught up with the little fucker. He wasn't so bad.

By the time we arrived at Reed's place, I had my head on straight enough that I could appreciate the impressive layout hidden behind what amounted to a goddamn forest. The security was state-of-the-art, unobtrusive enough that you couldn't see it if you weren't looking for it. We parked behind a steel fence that was at least ten feet tall with concrete woven through the grates. I followed Stitch up to a large industrial looking building. "Is this it?"

A laugh sounded a few feet away and I looked up to see who I guessed was Reed. He looked like a hippie with shoulder length brown hair and tons of gray around the edges. Worn jeans and a Traveling Wilburys' t-shirt covered his lanky frame and he topped the outfit off with a pair of Birkenstocks. "She's not much to look at but no, this isn't *it*." He held out his hand and wore a friendly smile. "Reed Henderson."

"Gunnar. Nice to meet ya."

He greeted Stitch with a handshake and a half-hug before guiding us on a tour of his operation. It included three different buildings for everything from cultivating flowers to production and storage. "Now *this* is it," he said with a proud smile I could appreciate. "What do you think?"

Both Stitch and Reed turned to me expectantly and I could admit the truth. "I think this is damn impressive, Reed." He ran a tight ship, taking every precaution necessary for the highest quality products and I respected the hell out of that. The dude was an old school hippie with a genius level IQ and a clear passion for weed. It was clear to see how he and Stitch had connected.

His smile grew bigger as he shoved hair from his face and smacked his hands together. "The only thing left to do is have a little toke."

"Or a big toke," Stitch added to what was clearly an inside joke.

Reed guided us along a path about a quarter-mile away from the buildings where a small creek bubbled between rocks. He sat down onto the grass and crossed his legs like some hippie yoga guru. Then he pulled out a vaporizer and a small glass pipe. "The vape will let you taste it pure but Stitch here is a heathen and prefers to torch the bud."

"Well I'd prefer a bong but I'm guessing it doesn't go with your sandals?" Stitch accepted the glass pipe with one hand and dug for a lighter with another.

I had to wait for the vaporizer to heat up which felt wrong and pretentious to me but when I took the first hit, I could admit, "This is damn good shit, man." Reed looked pleased but after that, I kind of zoned out, listening to the old friends catch up on life while I enjoyed my high.

"How's your girl?"

At Reed's question, Stitch shrugged. "Marisol is good but something is going on with her." I wasn't looking at Stitch but I could hear the worry in his voice, which probably would have made me worry if I hadn't been so stoned because when it came to chicks, the Reckless Bastards turned into Captain Save-A-Ho.

The silence, though momentary, was pensive before Reed spoke. "Be careful, Chris. She is a nice girl but she comes with shit you really don't want."

I heard the warning in Reed's words and he'd also used Stitch's given name, Chris. So I sat up. "What kind of shit?"

"Personal ones," the kid bit out with more force than I'd ever heard him use. It didn't make me feel any better about whoever this Marisol chick was.

"Right." If he thought I was done digging, then he was a bigger fool than I thought. I'd find the fucking answers before we got back to Mayhem.

"I'll leave you guys to enjoy the high. Find me before you go and I'll send you back with some bud." With the agility and speed of a man a decade younger, Reed got to his feet and whistled as he walked away.

Stitch was tense, bracing himself for the lecture he was so certain was coming. But I wasn't in the mood for a sermon. "Don't worry man, I'm saving my speeches for when Maisie is a teenage hellraiser."

"But?"

"But it never hurts to be careful in this life."

"You think I should steer clear of Marisol?"

I wanted to say hell yeah I thought so, but that would only send him running in her direction even faster. "That's not what I'm saying Stitch, but it's clear you don't know her. If you want her, find out her dark secrets before they bite you—and us—in the ass."

"So you're worried about yourself?"

I nodded because there was no fucking point in lying. "Me and the little girl under my care. Not to mention all the other women and kids." I stood so we were face to face, a few feet apart so he could hear me. Really hear me. "I never realized how fucking worrisome it was to be a parent Stitch, and if I had, maybe I would have had a better understanding of all the stress Cross has on his shoulders. It's something we all have to think about. But more importantly, if she needs help, you need to know so you can take it to Cross."

"She ain't my girl though, Gunnar. She's just a chick I spend some time with when I'm in the area."

I huffed out a laugh. "Since I doubt you told Reed what a good lay she is, I call bullshit."

Stitch let out a sigh and raked a hand through his long dark hair. "Do you mind if we make another quick stop?"

"Nah, let's go."

Reed loaded us up with product but it wasn't necessary. His shit was damn good and he had a professional operation that would make Cross happy. As soon as we got back, I'd give him my thoughts.

Thankfully when we got to Marisol's place, she wasn't at home.

Chapter Six - Jag

"Jag!" Rocky smiled up at me when she answered the door, Baby Dallas on her hip already reaching for me. "Sorry I didn't even hear the bell but I think Dallas has radar for his Uncle Jaggy!"

He leapt from her arms right into mine and I couldn't deny it felt good to be so welcome.

"Hey, kiddo!" He wrapped chubby little arms around me, babbling nonstop in his incoherent baby talk. "Sounds like there's a party going on inside."

"Of sorts," she said with a shrug before she stepped back. "The girls are hanging with me, Dallas and Maisie today. Come on in."

"Smells good in here." There were blankets and pillows all over the living room floor where the tiny humans played but mostly nibbled on fabric. And each other. The women were all gathered around the table in the dining room where they could keep an eye on the children while doing...whatever they were doing. "Hey ladies, how's it going?"

"Jag, did you come here to be our eye candy?" Teddy leaned forward, chin resting on her fist with a mischievous smile on her face.

Teddy was a troublemaker but she was also a stand up chick, willing to help whenever she could and always had a smart ass comment. "That's not why I came but look all you want." She opened her mouth and I pointed at her. "Just don't think anything is coming off."

Teddy pouted and sat back with a satisfied grin. "Wuss."

"Don't listen to her Jag," Jana pushed up from her seat with a soft smile and a shake of her silky blonde hair. "I'll get you something to eat *and* you can leave your shirt on."

"Bummer," Katrina muttered with a fake pout.

I had to shake my head at these women, so sassy all the damn time. Some of them, like Teddy and

Rocky, were always feisty as hell. But Jana had mostly been quiet and shy, keeping her steel hidden from everyone until it was necessary.

I'd known Katrina the longest since she ran Stetson for the MC, but usually she was the capable madam or house mother. Today she was just one of the girls. And they ran the men more than the men ran the club. But Jana could cook and that was why I was here. I was starved. "Gee, thanks Jana. And to think I was just telling Max what a good influence you are on him."

Her laugh echoed from the kitchen, sending Teddy and Rocky into a fit of giggles, which sent little Dallas off, laughing in my arms. "Damn right I am!"

"So what are you girls up to today besides causing trouble?" Scraps of fabric covered one end of the table. "Arts and crafts?"

"Shut your mouth!" Rocky's eyes went wide and her hands covered the materials and pens protectively. "For your information we're adding the finishing touches to all of the Halloween costumes for the kiddos. Both big and small." She arched a brow my way, daring me to diss her work.

"Please tell me you made Lasso a costume." Her smile said it all and I wanted to feel some excitement about Halloween and the dressed-up Bastards but couldn't find it in me.

"I don't know, Rocky, I think we have enough material to fashion some cowboy accessories for Jag." Teddy's eyes gleamed with an amusement that I didn't share.

"No thanks. This is more of a parent-child activity. And I am no one's baby daddy." Hell, I wasn't even sure if I was someone's man or not at this point. The room fell into a tense silence that any red-blooded man knew spelled *trouble*. And in a room full of known troublemakers, I was tempted to take Dallas and run like hell. But I was a hungry man and I'd sit here and eat the food Jana sat in front of me, and hope like hell they went easy on me. "Thanks, Jana."

"No problem. Eat up, big man." She plucked the baby from my arms with just a token protest from him and put him with the rest of the kids.

And eat was what I did, enjoying the stuffed chicken, asparagus and mashed potatoes. I was tempted to ask what occasion called for such a feast but I couldn't stop shoveling the food in my mouth. "So good."

"So," Rocky began with a relaxed grin. "When is Vivi coming back?"

Dammit. "Good question. If you find out, give me a call, would ya?" More than a week had passed since I'd last spoken to her, or received any kind of message. I didn't know if she was just busy—or in trouble.

"Shit, this just became a lot less fun," Teddy griped, wincing when Jana smacked her arm. "I mean, it sucks you don't know when she's coming back because now, teasing you just feels mean."

"Thanks Teddy. I wish she was already here and yeah, sometimes I wonder if she's ever coming back. I keep the faith. I might not get any answers and I have to be all right with that." The odds were astronomical that we'd get back together and now, with almost a year's absence, I worried I was asking too much.

"She'll be back Jag, don't you worry. I have a good feeling about you two." Rocky grinned and placed a gentle hand on top of mine.

I was glad one of us had a good feeling but I didn't say anything about it. Instead I smiled and turned to Jana and asked, "Got anymore of those mashed potatoes?"

I didn't want to talk about Vivi anymore and I didn't want to think about her right now either. I was more than content to hang around with the family I already had.

For now, anyway.

Chapter Seven - Stitch

Four days. Four fucking days since Gunnar and Cross had a closed-door meeting about doing business with Reed and I hadn't heard one single goddamn word. From either of them. It was total bullshit, stringing me along like this. I expected it from Gunnar, he was an old ass grouch, always complaining about shit instead of trying to enjoy what he had. A cute little girl and a club full of brothers who always had his back. Still he bitched and moaned. About everything.

But Cross not saying anything surprised me. So far, he had proven to be a great President despite all the shit we'd been through and all the stress he was under. And he'd always faced shit head on. Except this. It pissed me off, but I refused to show it, not when they still called me 'kid' and 'youngster' and anything else to remind me that I was years younger than all the older guys. And younger than some of the new prospects.

Instead, I stayed at home, inside my crappy little two-bedroom apartment. I didn't need or want more. Not yet. What I did want, though, was some food.

My fridge was bare so I grabbed my keys and headed for the door. At the same time a knock sounded. When I pulled the door open my jaw nearly fell to the floor at the sight of Marisol, all tan and curvy and luscious. And she looked scared. "Baby, what are you doing here? I'm so glad to see you. Come on in."

She sighed, wringing her hands. Those big brown eyes full of fear as she stepped in closer and wrapped her arms around me. "Stitch." Her voice came out on a shuddery whimper.

"Shit, babe. What's wrong?"

She held on tight for nearly a minute before sucking in a deep breath and letting it out. "Sorry." She stepped back on a shaky grin. "I just wanted to see you."

"As much as I want to believe that, I'm gonna have to call bullshit sweetheart." Everything about her screamed woman on the run and that had me on edge, blood pumping through my veins hot and thick like lava. Maybe it was the woman and her curves. Or maybe it was something else. I shut the door and said, "Come on, Marisol. Tell me what's going on."

She let me guide her to the sofa where she dropped down with a heavy sigh. "It's all so fucking cliché, Stitch."

"Tell me and our old friend Jack all about it," I said and poured two glasses of Tennessee's finest. "I assume this has to do with the married boyfriend?"

Marisol nodded and took two big gulps before she sank into the sofa with a sigh. "Yeah, who else?" She huffed out a bitter laugh and finished her glass before shoving it in my direction. "I woke up the day after your last visit to find Carlito sitting in my living room, drinking a cup of coffee. He sounded so fucking reasonable, the way he always did. At first."

A chill ran down my spine but I kept my mouth shut and listened. With a death grip on my glass. "And then?"

"Then he went totally fucking psycho. I walked straight past him and fixed a cup for myself and when I turned around, he was there like a creepy fucking turtle." She shivered at the memory. "His gaze narrowed and he looked at me with hate in his eyes before grabbing me by the throat. *You're mine, Marisol. You belong to me. Remember that,*" she repeated, mimicking a thick Spanish accent. "*You can fuck that white boy but don't ever forget, you are mine.*" She shoved her hair back, tucking some of the strands behind her ear so I could see her full face.

And the fucking bruise that was forming. "I'll fucking kill him."

Marisol's soft hand wrapped around my wrist and tugged. "I laughed at him. Told him that I'm his employee, one he forces to fuck." I opened my mouth to protest but she waved me off. "He backhanded me and for some reason I laughed even harder." The memory held her captive for a few seconds, her hands absently fidgeting with the hem of her tank top, her teeth nibbling her bottom lip. "He only proved my point and I told him as much. I'm stuck with him until one of us is dead but he likes to pretend it's a love match. Most days I can take it, but that morning I just couldn't let the charade go on, you know?"

Yeah, I fucking knew. "You can stay here, Marisol. As long as you need." No, that wasn't a good idea. "It might be better—"

"No, Stitch. Stop. I'm not here for your help."

I frowned. "And you're not here because you missed me, so what the hell, Marisol?"

"Carlito took my phone. That's why I haven't been in touch. Anyway he knows about you, I don't know how much but he knows and I had to warn you."

"I can handle myself, Marisol, but I appreciate your concern." I tried to pull her close, to offer her comfort but she pushed me away.

"Dammit, Stitch will you listen to me? He isn't just some shady businessman. It's Carlito Esteban, also known as *El Jefe*. He's the head of the Salinas Cartel."

Aww, shit. "Damn girl when you go big, you go big as hell don't you?" I needed a moment to think. If I was smart I would have called Cross but I quickly talked myself out of it. For now. "Is there anything you need from Reno? If not, we can grab some stuff from Target and I can get you out of town." It wasn't ideal but it was all I had at the moment.

She shook her head again, long thick hair spilling all around her shoulders. "I can't. There is no disappearing, not from them. Carlito will find me wherever I go. I have to go back."

"Okay. I'm going to Reno with you." I told her firmly, so she knew I wasn't asking.

"No, they'll kill—"

I held up a hand to stop her tirade when my phone began to vibrate across the coffee table.

It was Gunnar. "Yeah, what's up?"

"Cross gave the go ahead and he's already talked to Reed. We leave tomorrow at 0900 hours. Don't be late." He hung up like he always did. Rude fucker.

I turned back to Marisol. She looked even more scared than she had a minute ago. "The good news is that you'll have an escort home tomorrow."

Arms crossed, she narrowed her gaze in my direction. "And the bad news?"

I shrugged. "I don't *do* bad news sweetheart. The better news is that we get to break my bed tonight." The sound of her laugh, low and husky, was exactly what I wanted to hear in that moment.

"What about the couch, Stitch? Is it just the bed we get to break or can we try the couch too?"

I laughed and scooped her up in one arm and the bottle of Jack in the other. "If you're up for it, we can break the whole damn apartment."

KB WINTERS

Chapter Eight - Gunnar

Since I was the dumbass who had convinced Cross that this deal with Reed was a good one, I was determined not to be a jerk. But Stitch had a way of bringing out my innermost asshole. Like today when I knocked on his door only to be greeted by a curvy brunette who looked perfectly rumpled and well fucked. "Who the hell are you?"

"Marisol," she said, her chin hitched defensively. "Who the hell are you?"

"I'm the guy who's about to put a bullet in Stitch's ass. Stitch! Get your scrawny ass out here." If he wasn't ready to go, I'd head to Reed's place without him.

The door opened wider and the kid appeared, pulling a black t-shirt over his head and flicking long black hair that he really needed to cut. "Hey, Gunnar."

"Why the hell are you so surprised when I said nine in the morning?" A quick look at my watch said it was seven minutes til the hour. "Why aren't you ready?"

He wore that shit eating grin that made me want to punch his nose just to see it vanish, and raked a hand through his long damn hair that made me want to punch him twice. "We got a late start."

"Too fucking bad. We need to get on the road so I can get back. To Maisie, remember?" Ever since my mother died and I took custody of Maisie, I had the feeling that maybe the MC life wasn't for me. I loved my brothers and I'd come close to death on many occasions for them but shit like this made it hard to remember that. "This is your deal and today is the day it happens but you'd rather fuck around? You got five minutes or I'm gone. With or without you."

With a nod, Stitch stepped back and let me in. "We'll be ready. I promise."

I froze and glared at him. "We? No offense sweetheart." I took another glance at the pretty chick and turned back to Stitch. "We don't involve chicks in our business. Ever."

HOLIDAY HAVOC

"Give us a minute, will ya Marisol?" Stitch asked and she nodded and disappeared into one of the rooms down the hall, giving me time alone with the kid. "Look Gunnar, I know this isn't ideal but she's got this crazy ex and he's been stalking her. Showed up inside her apartment when she woke up and I couldn't let her go back, not last night."

"Cut the shit, Stitch. And tell me the goddamn truth. Tell me exactly what the fuck you're mixed up in. All of it. Be specific."

I knew he was nervous because of the way his hands kept raking through his hair. Yet when he spoke, I felt the blood drain from my body. Worse, I felt the tension seep under my skin and take hold of me, making me worry. Making me angry. "Jesus fucking Christ, Stitch! A cartel? A goddamn cartel. When you step in the shit, you step in it up to your waist, don't you?"

"It's nothing I can't handle," he insisted angrily and with a hint of that immature petulance that made new patches and prospects such a goddamn thorn in my side. "We just need to stop at Marisol's place on our way to Reed's."

"I swear to fuck—I could murder you with my bare hands right now dumb ass." I walked away from him and out of the apartment, whipping out my phone to dial Cross because this was something he needed to know. Every time one of the Reckless Bastards got involved with a Goddamn woman, she came with trouble.

Every fucking time.

"Yeah Cross, we've got a problem."

"Hey Gunnar, I can't really talk right now. Let me call you back in fifteen."

"I'll be on the road in...fuck!" He ended the call and it took every ounce of self-control I had not to smash my phone, go grab Maisie and keep driving until I ran out of gas. But I made a promise and unlike some people, I was a man of my word. "Goddammit!"

Three minutes later Stitch and his girl came strolling down the stairs like they were going to walk hand-in-hand around the county fair or some shit. Disgusted, I started my bike and peeled out of the parking lot ahead of them, eager to get away from this situation before I said or did something I couldn't take back.

My anger combined with my desire to get the fuck away from Stitch made the drive up to Reno fly by, mostly because I pushed the limits of speed the entire drive up. The whole morning had me wondering why the fuck I'd even bothered to come back to Mayhem. I'd never planned to once I knew Maisie was my responsibility.

But the Reckless Bastards were my family. Plus, I figured there was nowhere safer to raise my kid sister than surrounded by big bad bikers who'd protect her with their lives. Even the dumb shits like Stitch.

Since I wasn't a complete asshole, I stopped at the same rundown apartment building we'd stopped at the week before, and twenty minutes later, Marisol pulled her car in and Stitch parked his bike right beside her.

"Stay in the car," he barked and pointed my way. "Gunnar, a little help?"

"Aww, man. What the fuck is really going on? She can't go inside her fucking apartment now?" I knew I was being a dick but I couldn't help myself. "You think he's inside?"

"I think he could be in there, waiting for her."

I'd come across my fair share of crazy exes but something about this story didn't add up. Shit. "Stitch, tell me right now. Are you fucking a cartel boss's girlfriend?"

"The dude is married, Gunnar. Fucking married!"

"You really are a dumb son of a bitch who only thinks with his cock, aren't you? It doesn't matter if he's married. You know what this could mean for the club? For each and every one of us, including the women and children?" It was like he was trying to kick up as much shit as possible.

"It's too late for that. Let's just go and do a sweep of her place and then we'll be on our way."

HOLIDAY HAVOC

"A sweep? You watch too much TV, kid. And what if this is some goddamn setup by her? How well do you know her? She wouldn't be the first chick to create drama for fuckin' sport." I followed him up the concrete steps and waited while he opened the door.

Stitch stepped inside and I followed, coming to an abrupt fucking halt about five feet inside the small space. A small Hispanic man sat on the sofa in white pants and a light pink shirt with expensive looking cufflinks. If there had ever been any doubt about his identity there was a big ass 'S' on his belt buckle and the snakeskin cowboy boots were a dead fucking giveaway. "It's too bad you had to involve someone else in your theft."

"Theft? What the fuck are you talking about? I didn't steal anything, asshole." Stitch was all fired up and ready to fight because clearly, the dumb ass didn't notice the other four goons armed with automatic weapons, two on either side of us. Or he was too stupid to care.

"That's where you're wrong, *guerro*. Marisol is mine and you are trying to steal her from me."

"I wasn't until you went bat-shit crazy and broke into her apartment! Now, yeah I am."

"Goddammit man, shut the fuck up!" I ground out. This wasn't the time to get into a pissing match, not when they had us outmanned and outgunned. "Learn when to keep your fucking mouth shut."

Stitch glared at me. "What the fuck are you talking about??"

I spoke into Stitch's ear. "Look around, kid. Figure out what the fuck I'm talking about?"

"Listen to your friend and you might stay alive long enough to see another day." The guy was smarmy as fuck but he had that wild-eyed look of a man who wouldn't hesitate to fight dirty or kill for fun.

"Look, man I don't fight over chicks." Stitch had taken it down a notch. Being reasonable. "Not fucking ever, so tell me what you want."

HOLIDAY HAVOC

The guy sprang out of his seat. "Marisol is not just a *chick*, you imbecile! She is a beautiful woman and more importantly, she is mine. I will never let her go." I read the truth of his words all over his face. It was written in the upright way he held himself, shoulders squared and spine straight. The deadly ice in the depths of his gaze.

"Either way," I stepped forward in an effort to keep these assholes from beating the fuck out of each other. "He didn't know she belonged to someone else. It was an honest mistake."

"Bullshit!" He was barely five feet tall and looked more like an extra in a Telenovela than a big bad cartel boss. "He knew. You fucking knew." He pointed an accusing finger at Stitch, who leapt forward and threw a punch that sent the man falling backwards until he split the coffee table in half. "You are dead, motherfucker."

"Carlito, are you all right?"

So that was him. Carlito. "Get off me!" he snarled to his thugs helping him up. Once he was on his feet again, Carlito ordered, "Grab that asshole!"

All four men moved closer, weapons hanging loosely at their sides as they closed in on me and Stitch. "You don't want to do this," I warned them.

"*Si*, we do," one of Carlito's henchman said. The man was tall and thin and he looked like a brawler, which was good a good thing, because I was ready to fucking brawl.

He threw a punch. "Suit yourself," I said, ducking and rising with an uppercut that sent him flat on his back. I jumped on top of him, wailing on him with hammer fists until he was bloody and his eyes started to swell. A blow landed on my back and sent me flat on top of the other asshole.

Two sets of boots kicked and stomped on me, over and over again until I could barely take in a breath. I sure as shit couldn't look up without risking taking a boot to the head.

"Get up," one of the accented voices commanded and I took my sweet time. "I said get the fuck up!"

"I don't speak *Español* asshole!" I chuckled to myself when he started to pull me up, spitting some blood out on the unconscious asshole before I got to my feet. "Shit. Dick licker," I shouted when that piece of shit punched me right in the fucking side.

"You'll be licking dicks soon," he warned with more joy than I liked to hear following those words.

"The pink shirt was a dead giveaway that you fellas were on some gay shit."

"Gunnar!" Stitch's voice grabbed my attention for a brief moment. He was down on the floor with the remaining armed dickhead's foot on his chest.

"You okay?"

"Been better but he hits like a bitch."

I smiled at the little smart ass and slid one hand into my pocket, reaching for my blade. Carlito stood again, glaring at all of us. "You're outnumbered."

"Not by much," I told him with confidence. "Why don't you tell us what the fuck you want, Carlito?"

"There are four of us and two of you." He grinned and took a step forward but froze in his path when I flexed in his direction. "Keep this *puto* away from me!" His order was part fear and part anger.

The asshole to my right grabbed the back of my shirt, leaving his body exposed which gave me the perfect opportunity to act. The blade came out of my pocket and I jammed it into that motherfucker's neck.

I let go of the man, taking my blade with me. Blood squirted all over the fucking place as his eyes widened in shock and he smacked one hand over the hole in his neck. He tried to sputter out a few words, but he was bleeding out too quickly and once he fell to his knees, I knew it was over for him. "I think that puts it at three against two unless this guy right here wants to be a hero."

"Gunnar, watch—" Stitch's voice rang out, but I didn't hear his warning because something hard

HOLIDAY HAVOC

crashed down on the back of my skull and everything went fucking dark.

Chapter Nine - Cross

"Ewww, you guys are always kissing!" Beau's disgusted groan tugged a smile across my lips as they pressed against Moon's. "Come on!"

Moon stepped back, fingertips to her lips like she was trying to keep the heat of the kiss right on those plump lips I loved to taste. "I can't wait to remind you of this moment when you finally realize how amazing girls are."

Beau shrugged and pushed his glasses up on his nose. "I like girls but kissing is gross. Are you done?"

I smiled at the kid and winked. "Almost." Before she realized what I had in mind, Moon was in my arms, her lean curves flush against my body, hard and aching despite the pint-sized audience. I lowered my head to hers with a wide smile before our lips touched.

"Gross!" Beau's pout didn't deter me this time, not when Moon's tongue slicked across my bottom lip and not when she opened up and gave me a taste of the apple and cinnamon pie she'd eaten earlier. "Stop it, please!"

Eventually I put the kid out of his misery and pulled back, but I couldn't let Moon go. I wouldn't. Not now that I'd finally started living again and it was all because of her. "Only because you asked so nicely, kid."

"Is lunch ready yet? I'm hungry." Beau was always hungry but he was as scrawny as a grasshopper and I had no fucking clue where he put it all.

"Didn't we just eat breakfast?"

Beau stomped over to me with a serious look on his face as he tried to climb my leg, his favorite activity when he wanted to feel tall. "Mama says I'm a growing boy and I need my vitamins!"

I looked at her with an arch to my eyebrows. "So you're to blame for this behavior?"

Moon's face lit up beautifully, the way it always did when Beau and I were together. She never said a thing, but the pure joy she felt was written all over her face. Her hair was loose, spilling around her shoulders and back, over her blue and pink and purple dress that cupped her tits and highlighted her strong arms. "If you're asking am I responsible for the world's greatest son, the answer is yes."

"Thanks, Mama. You're the best too." She leaned in and kissed his cheek and I couldn't help but smile at my little family.

"What about me?"

Moon pressed her lips to my cheek and, unsurprisingly, Beau did the same thing on the other side. "We think you're the best too, Cross, don't we, Beau?"

Beau nodded. "Yeah. We love you, Cross."

Damn, how in the hell did a kid barely able to take care of himself get to me? I couldn't answer that, but the way his big blue eyes were filled with love and affection made me realize how ready I was for this. Love. Family. "I love you guys, too."

"Now that we have that settled, wash your hands and grab the dishes. We're eating in the backyard."

Moon loved her backyard and we'd spent the better part of the past year turning it into even more of an oasis than it had been. There were more flowers and a larger vegetable garden, a bigger table so she could entertain her new crop of girlfriends. My favorite was the hammock where I loved curling my body around hers and watching the stars.

It was sappy as hell, I knew it, and I also knew if the guys saw me they would tease me relentlessly. "I'll grab the dishes and you can set the table," I told Beau and he darted off to wash his hands.

"Thanks for watching him this week, though I wonder if I should be thanking you." With a hand to my chest, she smiled up at me with love in her eyes. "The fact that he hasn't stopped talking about it means you probably gave him tons of junk, let him stay up late and watch scary movies."

"I plead the fifth," I told her and planted another kiss behind her ear, pants tightening at the way she sighed and leaned into me. The phone vibrating in my pocket pulled us apart. "Hang on, babe," I said reluctantly as I answered it.

"Hey Cross, it's Reed. I just want to see if you'd changed your mind about doing business together. No hard feelings if you have, but I need to know."

"Is this some kind of bullshit, Reed? Because this isn't how I do business." Moon's fingers dug into the tension hardening my shoulders and it felt so fucking good I wanted to groan.

"No, it's not bullshit. I expected Chris and Gunnar yesterday afternoon but I haven't seen them. I called Chris, but he didn't answer and that's not like him. I don't have time for this. I have a business to run."

Shit, that wasn't like Stitch. Despite his youth and sometimes over-eagerness, he was as solid as they came. "My bad, Reed. But fuck, I expected them to be on their way back here by now."

Reed fell silent. I had to remind myself he wasn't part of the MC and was probably freaking out right now.

"I know he's been seeing a girl in Reno, Cross, but all I know is that her name's Marisol. I wish I could be more helpful."

"That's a good start, Reed. I need to find my men first but I want to make this deal happen. Do you think you might find your way down near Mayhem anytime soon?"

"I'll let you know. And please, let me know when you hear from Chris."

"Will do, man. Thanks." I ended the call and a string of profanities ran through my mind, enough that it would've made Moon blush. "Fuck!"

"Tell me what's wrong." Moon's soft voice was right by my ear, her tits pressed against my back as she wrapped her arms around my waist.

"It's Gunnar and—"

"Mama, Aunt Rocky is here!" Beau was over the moon about all the new kids in his life. I thought it was because he got to be the older and wiser cousin but

Moon believed it was just happiness at more friends to play with.

Rocky walked into the back yard, pink t-shirt falling off one shoulder while her cut-off shorts showed miles and miles of leg. Maisie held one hand and Dallas held the other, at least until he caught sight of Moon with all her colorful patterns and noisy jewelry. "Gunnar never showed up," she said with an angry pout but I could see the lines of tension and fear around big green eyes.

"Yeah, something is up." I didn't know what, not yet, but I had a feeling it was nothing good. "Shit!" All I wanted was one full year with no drama. No bullshit. No more beefs. But that was too much to ask. I dialed Jag but I wasn't surprised when he didn't answer so I tried Savior next and informed him of our missing brothers.

"Shit. I'll round up the guys. What else?"

"Rocky and Moon are with me so I'll get them to the clubhouse but we need to check their places. Take one of the prospects with you to Gunnar's and I'll send Max to Stitch's place."

"Got it." Savior ended the call and I let out a long, deep breath. The shit was happening again. If it wasn't one thing, it was another. When I looked up, Moon and Rocky had worried looks while Beau had taken the other kids away to play. "We don't know anything yet, ladies except no one has heard from them or seen them since early yesterday."

Rocky moaned. "Fuck. Another lockdown? If you guys keep this up, I'm going to have to start grocery shopping for the clubhouse because your food choices suck." That was a fair complaint and I responded with a shrug.

"Don't worry, we're gonna eat first and then pack. Then go." Meal time with Moon and Beau was one of my favorite parts of the day. As long as all the women were safe, I could relax. A little.

Long enough to eat anyway.

But eventually meal time ended and it was time to get serious again. The clubhouse was abuzz with activity when I escorted Moon and Rocky through the doors, three kids in tow. It had taken us two hours to pack everything three small humans would need from their respective houses, and get us all over here, but now it was done.

"Sit tight girls and hopefully we'll have some answers soon." I didn't believe it, though, and based on the sympathetic smile Moon sent me and the way her green eyes glittered with worry, I knew she was trying to help.

"We'll be fine, Cross. Go take care of your guys."

"Damn I love the hell out of you, my crazy little hippie." I stole another kiss because when her sweet lips called to me, dared me to resist them? I failed.

Every fucking time.

"Good because I love you too. Now go." She smacked my ass when I turned to walk away, pulling another laugh from me.

"I love you, now go? That's a new one."

That thick, husky laugh sounded again. "How else will I keep you on your toes?"

She didn't need to do anything but be herself to keep me on my toes and she damn well knew it. Between her biting wit and odd sense of humor, there was never a dull moment with Moon around. "You'll just have to be more creative," I taunted before stepping inside Merry Mayhem and shutting the door behind me. All eyes were on me. All of the Reckless Bastards were gathered in this space, created just for us, and waiting for my instruction on how we would find our brothers. "Okay, what do we know?"

Max stood to give us the news, his expression grave. "Nothing for sure. Black and I went over to Stitch's place and it was empty. Nothing was out of place or turned over so we assume they got on the road." Max's hands flexed and clenched tight, a sure sign that he was pissed the fuck off. It was a Max none of us had seen much of since he met Jana, but right now he was ready to tear someone's head off.

"Well, that's something." I said. "Reed said something about a girl he was seeing, anyone know anything about that?"

Lex's thick ginger hair fell over his eyes when he stood and he blew out a breath before he spoke. Worried? Pissed. Hard to tell. He said, "I know *about* her and that she lives in Reno but that's about it. He never even said her name, but he did tell me she had tits like a Barbie and she fucked like a porn star." Lex's words drew a few knowing laughs from around the table because that sounded exactly like Stitch.

"Fuck. Since when is Stitch so fucking tight-lipped?" The kid was the king of the goddamn overshare.

Max let out a heavy sigh and dropped down into his seat beside Savior. "Dodds came to see me at Get Ink'd. He came to ask if the Reckless Bastards were doing business with cartels. He had a specific cartel in mind but he didn't say which one."

"Cartels?" Savior asked.

Max nodded. "He seemed unusually worried and he only came in for info which I didn't have."

"This can't be a fucking coincidence." If it was we had to be the unluckiest club on the fucking planet. "We need to find out which cartel it was and we need to find out more about this Marisol chick. Fuck! Where the fuck is Jag?"

Max shrugged. "He left the shop when his shift was over but he's not answering his phone."

I knew he was in a funk and I of all people understood what he was going through, but goddammit now was not the time. "Find him. Now."

Chapter Ten - Jag

I sat inside my house with all the blinds drawn shut so that not an ounce of sunlight could sneak inside, wallowing like a fucking baby. I should just shake it off. Hell, losing Vivi—which was clearly what the fuck was going on—wasn't even the worst thing that had ever happened to me. I'd lost both of my parents before I made it to adulthood, not to mention all the brothers I'd lost in the service.

This should be small fucking potatoes in comparison. I was alive and well. Should've been grateful for the air I breath.

But I wasn't. No, I was wallowing in pity because Vivi wasn't here. I hadn't heard from her, either.

It really pissed me off that once again, the government had taken someone from me. It was bullshit but it was also becoming clear to me that I needed to find a way to get over it. To get used to living without her.

I lived without her for years, and I could do it now.

And the perfect recipe for forgetting was an expensive bottle of Maker's Mark Vivi had sent last month. I was four shots in when the bell rang and with an angry grunt, I got up to open the door.

"Delivery for Jeremiah Washington." The kid couldn't have be more than eighteen with that lanky frame and the last traces of adolescent acne.

"Yeah, that's me." I signed for the package, accepted it and kicked the door shut in the kid's face. The box was relatively small and I opened warily since I hadn't ordered anything, and there was only one person other than my mom who called me Jeremiah.

That reminder spurred me on, hope swelled inside as I pulled out my knife and sliced through the tape until the flaps swung open, yanking a hard laugh from me.

Inside the box was a small bag of pretzels, a pair of horn-rimmed glasses, a black tie and a pair of black Speedos. That was it. No note or instructions. Typical

Vivi. I smiled and tossed it on an end table and dropped back down on the sofa, turning back to watching crazy YouTube videos on the TV, trying not to think about her. It made me feel better to see people more fucked up than me right now.

The fucking doorbell rang again.

"What?" I yanked the door open and it was the same fucking kid.

"Sorry sir, this one was separate." He handed me a smaller box this time, about the size of a jewelry box.

"Thanks, kid. Got anything else?" He face turned pink and he shook his head before turning around and racing down the steps. "Good." When I tore the small box open I barked out another laugh at the cheesy gold painted CIA badge. Vivi was nuts but as long as she wasn't here, this was just a tease and I tossed it with the rest of the costume. I wondered if she'd call soon. I needed to hear her voice.

The doorbell chimed again a few minutes later and I about lost my shit the way the Russian drivers on my screen were. "What the fuck?" I yanked the door open and froze.

"Not exactly the greeting I was hoping for. Maybe we should try this again?"

"Damn." Vivi stood on my doorstep, blue hair now pink, which made her gray eyes look like melted silver. But my eyes were drawn to the skin tight orange jumpsuit that hugged her long legs and sensual curves exactly the way I wanted to.

"What's with the jumpsuit?"

Her eyes lit with mischief as she licked her lips and slipped past me. "I'm a bad girl, don't you know? Been serving my time with government suits, keeping me away from my hot chocolate."

I laughed again and shut the door. Locked it too. Twice. "Hot chocolate?"

She nodded, and I wrapped her in my arms. All the anger floating away as I held her. I breathed in her scent. "Damn, girl, I missed you."

"I missed you too, lover boy." She stepped back a little and released a few of the snap buttons on her jumpsuit, revealing a bra that cupped her tits like a pair of hands. The bra had black and white prison stripes. "You're *hot* as fuck and pure fucking *chocolate*, Jeremiah Washington."

The way my name rolled off her tongue was just what I wanted to hear. Her words woke my cock right up, but she wasn't done, snatching the buttons open all the way down to her belly button and pushing them over her hips to show off a tiny pair of panties. In matching prison stripes. "You have been a bad girl, Vivi. Keeping me waiting for you." I took a step forward and she put her hands on her hips, daring me.

"They say absence makes the heart grow fonder. Are you *fonder*?" Her voice was shaky and low.

"Fuck, yeah, I'm *fonder*. Are you here for good?" God, I was the happiest man alive. "Don't answer that, I don't want to know."

Our lips were barely an inch apart, stares glued to each other and I watched in fascination as her silver eyes turned a dark gunmetal color. "I was starting to think I'd have to live on nothing but anticipation."

Her breath hitched as she waited a second. And finally, she let out a sigh. "Do I get a welcome home kiss?"

I dared her with nothing but a look. That one look was all it took for Vivi to launch herself at me and slam her mouth against mine. The kiss started out hard and fast and intense, the kiss of lovers separated for too damn long but slowly, eventually she slowed the pace and savored my mouth. Savored the taste like a starving woman who'd finally gotten a slice of her favorite dessert. She clung to me like she was afraid I might break the kiss, break our sweet connection.

As if I could. I held on to her, gripping her hips and her ass to fix her against me just the way we both wanted. Needed. I held her close and let her devour my mouth while my hands got reacquainted with lean muscles covered with soft, feminine curves. My feet began to move with the intention of laying her out on my bed and spending the rest of the week making her scream my name but my brain had other thoughts.

The bed's too fucking far.

Instead we landed on the sofa, my body covering hers until she reached for me and wrapped her legs around my waist. "Someone's happy to see me."

"Yeah, all of me is so fucking happy to see you, babe." She smiled a soft feminine smile that seemed so unlike her but never failed to make me feel like a goddamn superhero. "So damn happy."

"Me too, Jag. Me too." She nibbled my chin and licked a trail of heat from my collarbone up to my ear. "And I promise to say all the sappy shit about how much I missed you but right now, I need you. I need this. Right. Now." Her words were punctuated with sharp, choppy moves as her hands made quick work of the button and zipper on my jeans and her hand went inside, wrapping around my dick. "Fuck, I've missed your cock."

She laughed when my dick twitched in her hand and I repaid the favor, yanking the black and white panties off her body to reveal a freshly bare pussy with a tiny J in pale blond hair. "Fuck, Vivi."

"That's the idea. Just in case, you know, there was any doubt."

It was so goddamn hot and so typically Vivi. I rolled off the sofa and onto my knees. "Just in case *you* forgot." I spread her wide, loving the way her glistening pussy clenched with need, the way she was already leaking with just a look. Then my mouth was on her, savoring the taste of her juices on my tongue.

"Oh fuck, Jag! Yes!" She was as hungry for this as I was, a fact that made me happier than I would ever admit to anyone but her. I shoved my tongue inside her pussy because she loved it when I fucked her with my mouth. "Yes, baby, yes!" Her hips writhed and swirled, her hands went to my head, holding me still while she rubbed herself against me. "Oh fuck. Oh God, Jag. Yes. More."

I smiled against her, loving when my girl was bossy. It was her default and I hadn't realized until that moment how much I missed her bossy side. Then I gave her what she wanted, pulling her swollen clit between my lips and nibbling it with my teeth.

"Jag!" Her orgasm was close. So fucking close I could feel the way she trembled beneath me. Her body shook more and more violently as her orgasm slowly came to the surface and she strained to reach for that pleasure that eluded her. "Goddammit, Jag!"

Then, when she was so blind with frustration she couldn't talk, could only scream and moan, I licked and sucked her sweet clit. Hard and fast, soft and slow. Good enough to put any vibrator to shame. She came hard, in waves as her long-awaited orgasm slammed through her and I didn't let up. I slid two fingers inside her pulsing cunt, rubbing her g-spot until her juices hit my chin like a tsunami. Her orgasm ratcheted up a notch or two—or ten. She cried out my name over and over again until she was spent.

"Damn Jag. Damn."

"Welcome home, baby."

She sighed with a sated smile and slowly turned until her head hung over the edge of the sofa. "Now I need a taste." Without any other prompting she opened her mouth, legs spread wide so I could see her pussy, still clenching and pulsing from her orgasm and I gave her what she wanted. "Mmm."

"Ah, shit!" The feel of her wet lips wrapped around my cock, the vibrations of her moans hit me right in the nuts. My hips began to pump in the rhythm that she mirrored. "Suck it." She swiped a tongue around the head of my cock until my hips jerked, sending my cock straight down her throat. "Yeah, just like that." Her hands went to my ass, setting a fast rhythm I knew would send me off in seconds.

The sounds of her moaning around my cock, the way her nails dug into my ass, the scent of her pussy still damp and hungry for me, it was all too much. I leaned forward, licking her pussy and fucking her mouth, causing too many sensations for me to do anything but suck her clit to orgasm while she swallowed my load. "You really are my hot chocolate, baby." She smacked my ass and gave me one last lick that buckled my legs and sent me collapsing on the floor.

I couldn't help but laugh. "Fuck me, I'm so happy you're back. You are back, aren't you?"

"I am. For as long as you want me," she said and rolled off the couch, right on top of me. "You still want me here, right? Or did I wait too long?" I could barely hear her question with the way her slick pussy slid up and down my shaft, already growing hard again and hungry for her.

"It was too fucking long but now that you're here," I gripped her hips hard and thrust up against her, pulling a low moan from her, "I'm keeping you. Forever."

A soft smile touched her lips even as her hips continued to grind against me. "Forever is a mighty long time. Maybe that's just the sex talking?"

Fuck that. I wrapped an arm around her waist and flipped our positions, quickly slipping back inside her hot, wet pussy. "It's not the fucking sex, but I'm happy to prove it." Before she could say another word, I flipped her legs over my forearms and squeezed her hips to keep her right where I wanted as I plunged in and out of her, with a blind need that felt like it would never ever be satisfied. I thrust and pounded, her moans and cries just the thing I needed to send heat skittering up and down my sweat slicked body.

"Jag! Oh fuck, oh fuck!" She was close again and yeah, that knowledge only made me fuck her harder. Deeper. With more intensity than I'd ever fucked anyone in my life. "Jag! Fuck!"

My mouth crashed down on hers, swallowing her cries of pleasure until she clenched around my cock and pulled another orgasm from me. I shook and trembled before collapsing on top of her. "Forever ain't gonna be enough, Vivi."

Her legs tightened around me, reluctant to let me go. "Maybe not, but it's a good fucking start."

"Jesus fuck, no wonder he hasn't been answering his phone!" Savior's voice cut through the emotion in the room. "Hey Vivi."

She arched her back and looked at Savior and Max with a grin. "Hey guys, how's it going?"

"No. No, no, no. We are not about to shoot the breeze while I'm still inside her. Give us a minute, yeah?"

Savior grinned and continued to stare even as Max pulled him into the kitchen. "No point in locking the front if you forget about the back," he called out, laughter ringing in his voice.

I looked down at Vivi. "Sorry about that."

"Don't be. I'm too happy to care. Honestly I could fuck you again. Right now." She clenched around me just to prove her point. "But I'm guessing whatever brought those guys here is important."

It always fucking was. With great reluctance, I slowly separated our bodies and grunted. "Yeah." I didn't know what was going on but clearly it was serious for the guys to interrupt me. I slid my pants back on and went to the kitchen. "What's up?"

"We got a problem," Savior began. "Gunnar and Stitch never made it up to Reed's place."

"Shit." The word came out on an exhale. "So they're missing? Did you check their places?"

"Are you really asking us that? Of course we did. Everything looked normal so we assumed they headed up that way," Max said, troubled. "Apparently Stitch has a girl up in Reno but all we got is a first name. Marisol."

Okay. I could work with that. "All right. I'll get their phones tracked and see what I can find."

Vivi strolled in, a laptop in her hand and still wearing her orange jumpsuit. "What can I do to help?"

Savior's lips twitched. "Tell us about the jumpsuit."

"Roleplaying," she said simply and looked up. "We gonna talk about the hot sex we just had or do you want help finding your buddies?"

I kissed her cheek and smiled at the guys. "You heard her."

Savior leaned on his elbows. "Jag, you can find the buddies while she tells us all about this hot sex."

"It would be unfair to make you feel inadequate," she told him, her gaze never leaving the computer screen. "There are three Marisol's in Reno."

The kitchen fell silent for a long moment and then we all got to our feet. "Give us ten minutes to get dressed and we'll meet you at the clubhouse."

When we were alone, Vivi slipped outside and came back with clothes across her arm. "I left them in my camper, which I'm happy to see you still have. But we have a problem."

"We do?"

She nodded. "I need a shower and you told the guys ten minutes," she said, two fingers traveling slowly down her body, between her tits and down to the hot sweetness sticking to her thighs.

"Then I guess we'll just have to be quick about it." I breathed.

Thirty minutes later we were headed to the clubhouse.

Chapter Eleven - Gunnar

Fuck, my head hurt like a motherfucker. It throbbed so hard, so damn loud I couldn't even tell where I was. It was dark. "What the fuck?"

"Gunnar?" Stitch's voice rang out in the pitch black room but he sounded far away, or maybe it had something to do with the tennis ball sized knot on the back of my head. "Shit man, I thought you were fucking dead."

"Glad to see you came to my defense, kid. Why are the fucking lights out?" I tried to push up off the ground and that was when I felt my ribs. Where I'd been kicked, and hard plastic cutting into my wrists. The hard plastic like fucking zip ties. "What the hell is going on, Stitch?" I may not have been the smartest tool in the damn shed but nothing about this felt right.

"You don't remember?"

A low growl escaped, frustration or maybe anger, I didn't know. Maybe both. "Would I be asking if I did?"

"Right." Stitch took a deep breath and I listened in equal parts horror and anger as he reminded me about the un-fucking-necessary pitstop at his girlfriend's apartment and her married boyfriend. "We fought, and you killed one of his men before you took the butt of a 9 mil to the back of the head and we ended up here."

Here seemed to be a cold slab of concrete in a dark room, which didn't tell me much. "Shit, I killed somebody? I hope that fucker deserved it. Any idea where here is?"

"Some fucking warehouse but I don't know where." The frustration in his voice was about the only damn thing that could have doused the anger threatening to spill out of me. "I was out for a long damn time, too. I think that crazy fucker chloroformed me. I woke up about an hour ago."

Shit. That meant he knew about as much as I did, which was to say not a goddamn thing. "Anyone been in here?"

HOLIDAY HAVOC

"Not since I first woke up. Some short Hispanic dude came in and dropped a few bottles of water between us, maybe three feet toward my voice."

I felt like I had cottonmouth, in addition to the biggest goddamn headache I'd ever had so I pushed myself up into a sitting position and tried to orient myself. Even in a black room, it spun from my movements. "Fuck that must've been one blow to the head."

"It was," Stitch confirmed. "You were on the ground and the pussy stood right above you."

I listened to Stitch with a sinking feeling in my gut. As he talked about the fight, it all came back to me. The blood squirting from the asshole's neck as he went down. Stitch knocking that little pissant Carlito to the ground. "Fuck." These goddamn zip ties were a fucking problem and I wasn't flexible enough to reach for my blade.

"If you're looking for help with these fucking flexi-cuffs, good luck. They're tight as shit and your blade is back at Marisol's place."

Marisol. Even the sound of her name pissed me right the fuck off. If not for her, and if not for Stitch's inability to keep his cock zipped up, I'd be at home with Maisie right now. "This is your fucking fault, Stitch, I need you to know that. To hear me and really fucking let that sink in because when we get out of here, I'm gonna fuck you up." He stayed silent like the kid he was and I grunted. "But right now, we have to figure a way out of this shit."

"We can't do shit in this fucking place. I was so damn thrilled at first, thinking they'd be easy to get off since they tied us up in the front, but we're good and fucking stuck."

That was where he was wrong. Though I would never admit this to the kid, or anyone for that matter, I'd spent a lot of time watching bullshit videos on YouTube while I was sitting around waiting for my mom to die. Some of it—crazy Russian drivers, epic fails and motorcycle fights—was useless, but some of those videos turned out to be pretty damn helpful. I'd renovated mom's place on my own before putting it on the market with the help of a few at home DIY'ers and now I would get us out of this mess as well.

"It's a good thing I don't plan on keeping these fucking things on for long."

"You keep a blade under your nut sac or something?"

He was being a smartass while I was concentrating on trying to remember what I saw in that damn video at four o'clock in the morning. I rose to my feet figuring it would give me better leverage and pulled the little tail until my fingers started to tingle. Then I lifted my hands over my head and brought those motherfuckers down against my tightened stomach with all the force I could, and the hard plastic snapped down the middle. "No, asshole, I keep a brain in my fucking skull. You ready to get the fuck outta here?"

Just then, the door opened and a large slice of light spilled in, silhouetting two figures in the doorway. "Be cool," I whispered to Stitch and slid back to my spot, knocking over the remaining bottles of water in the process, goddammit. We needed any advantage we could get against these assholes and clearly it was up to me to find it.

One guy walked in with two bags and tossed them on the floor. Thankfully he set the takeout cups down with a bit more finesse. While he dealt with the food, the other one held a gun trained on us, an M4 Carbine favored by the most brutal of the cartels. "Eat."

"No onions?" Stitch asked in his trademark smartass.

"Eat, *puto*." The little fucker turned with a smirk and left us again, in the goddamn dark. Apparently, he expected us to pick up our food in the dark, grabbing it with the cuffs on.

"So what's your great idea?" Stitch's mouth would get him in trouble one day and I could only hope I wasn't caught in the blast zone when it did.

I saw him grabbing for the food and went over to him, smacking the burger out of his hand. "Don't eat that shit, you don't know what they did to it. Stand up."

"I'm not gonna fight you, Gunnar."

"I know that, stand the fuck up." When he finally did what I asked, I showed him how to get out of his zip ties.

"Holy shit, it worked!"

I couldn't help but smile at his enthusiasm. "We're going to find a way out of this place," he blurted out.

It was hard to forget that compared to most of us, Stitch was little more than a kid. I took a few deep breaths to calm myself because I couldn't keep snapping at him even if this was completely his fucking fault.

"Keep quiet. We need to look around and see where we are, find something to use as weapons and figure out how to get the fuck outta here."

He waited a beat until my words sank in, then he gave a sharp nod. "Got it."

We were definitely inside some kind of warehouse because there were boxes and barrels every few feet. I couldn't see for shit, but I knew that because every fucking time I turned, I collided with something, which meant it took a long damn time before I got to a wall with a few windows. About fifteen feet above my six-foot-four frame.

"Fuck," I muttered. I'd have to be a body builder to hoist myself up to that window. I just wanted to see where the hell that crazy Mexican had taken us.

"Gunnar!" Stitch's voice came out in a harsh whisper that was barely audible across the expansive room. I couldn't see him but I moved toward his voice, careful not to knock over anything or make any noise that would send those fuckers running in here.

"What did you find?" I asked when I finally reached him. He pointed up and followed the path of his finger to a window. It was only about six feet above us, but it couldn't have been more than two feet wide and one foot thick which meant neither of us could fit through it. "Shit."

"I know," he shot back with frustration in his voice. "Just get your old ass up there and look outside."

HOLIDAY HAVOC

There was an urgency to his voice I'd never heard before. I knew before I hoisted myself up on the rickety desk and wiped away some of the dust that covered the window that whatever this place was, it wasn't used regularly. At least this spot wasn't because under my foot was a layer of dust that made it hard for my boots to grip.

The window was twice as filthy, but when I squinted my eyes to readjust to the lights outside, I froze. Right across the street was a strip mall with a laundromat, some kind of greasy spoon diner, a grocery store that was the only establishment without any lights and a lawyer's office.

"It's in fucking Spanish!"

"I know, I hear them talking." Stitch said. "All Spanish with no hint of English," he explained carefully like I was a goddamn idiot who needed to have things explained to me. "We must be somewhere in Mexico."

Somewhere in Mexico. "Fucking Mexico." That couldn't be a good sign. There was only one reason I could think of why Carlito would bring us here. "We have to get the fuck out of here. Now."

"Damn straight. That crazy fucker isn't letting us leave here alive."

The door slammed open again and then a familiar voice sounded. "Oh good, you're awake."

I'd fought in the government's wars, did more tours than I ever wanted to fucking think about again and killed more men—and a few children—who were just like me, caught up in some rich man's web of greed and power. But watching Carlito in that doorway, backlit with blinking fluorescent lights, I finally understood what people meant when they said pure evil.

Chapter Twelve – Golden Boy

"Fuck man, it feels good to get a win!" I shouldn't have been as excited as I was but it felt damn good to take home, not just the top prize which was fifty grand but we'd also taken home the prize for most innovative techniques and design for some of the 3D designs Lasso had done for a few celebrities breezing through Vegas.

"Damn right it does," Lasso whooped as he turned into my driveway and put the car in park. "Thirty-two G's ain't a bad haul for a week of work!"

I frowned. "Dammit Lasso, I told you that you're keeping the fifteen thousand for yourself and don't act like you can't use it. The way you and Rocky go at it, she'll be pregnant again in no time." Whenever I called or stopped by, they were going at it or had just finished. Hell, they'd be making eyes at each other even before me and Teddy were gone.

"What can I say? My stamina is legendary and my wife can't get enough of me." He flashed his wide, cowboy grin before stepping out of the truck. "I can give you a few pointers if you'd like."

"My man exceeds all expectations in the bedroom, thank you very much." I smiled as I looked up and caught sight of my wife in her long-legged, curvaceous glory. Standing on the porch in a pair of denim shorts and a thin tank top that our daughter tugged on with her chubby little hands, revealing Teddy's red lace bra that had my mouth watering. My cock twitched for her.

"Thanks babe, but I don't need to prove shit to Lasso." He barked out a laugh because the man was incapable of being offended. "He knows what a big strong man I am."

Teddy arched an eyebrow in my direction, her lips twisted into a sexy little smirk I couldn't wait to kiss. She'd just applied that shiny fruity shit I loved so much to her lips, like she was waiting for me to come home and kiss it off of her. "Does he now? Anything you want to tell me about what happened in LA?" Her blue eyes sparkled with mischief. With joy and I knew, without a doubt, both were due to me.

I smiled and climbed another step, so we were eye to eye. "Yeah, but not while there are tiny ears around."

"Daddy!" As my voice grew closer, it stirred our little girl in Teddy's arms and she popped up with a wide baby-toothed grin.

"Hey, Princess. How's Daddy's little girl?" She giggled and squirmed in her mother's arms, eager to get into mine where she could count on a few tosses into the air and a big fat raspberry on her little belly.

"Hi Daddy!" The sound of her laughter was what I lived for. It, more than anything, had revived me. Meeting Teddy had brought me back to life but Quinn, my beautiful little girl? She was what kept me going. Every morning I woke up and remembered how lucky I was to meet the fiery former model with balls of steel, and to have the greatest baby girl in the world.

"Did you miss me?"

Instead of answering, Quinn nodded hard and closed her eyes, puckering up for a kiss. "Sugar!" I gave her what she wanted but soon, too damn soon, she was distracted by the big blond cowboy at my side. "Cowboy!"

"Well hey there, sugar." He winked, charming even the littlest of women and I didn't even mind when she reached for him because it gave me a moment to greet my wife in peace.

"Hey babe." I wrapped one arm around her waist and tugged her closer, inhaling her expensive floral scent. "You smell good."

Her laugh came out deep and husky as she threw her arms around me, fingers playing lightly in my long blond hair. "Hey back. Miss me?"

"So fucking much." The words came out on a growl. Guttural and primal, just like my desire, my need for her. "I can't wait to show you. Later." In that moment, all I needed was a quick taste of plump pink lips that tasted like watermelon and Teddy. A perfect fucking combination. The kiss started out soft, both of us pretending that we gave a fuck about things like decency and manners, before it kicked up a notch or ten and turned into flat out hotness. Our kisses were always intense, sharp with raw need and then grew into a frenzy of lips and teeth, tangling tongues, grunts, moans and groans. I couldn't get enough, sucking her tongue while her fingers tightened in my hair.

Lasso cleared his throat and after a few seconds, okay maybe a few minutes, I was able to pull myself from my wife's succulent lips. "Mmm, remember where we were later."

I adjusted my pants while her body was still pressed against mine before letting her take a step up. "Like I could forget."

"I thought you were coming right back in." Savior stood in the doorway of my home, arms crossed while he scowled at my wife.

Teddy, shrugged, looking completely unmoved by his tone. "I was coming back in but have you ever been kissed by this man?" Her lips twitched as she fought the laughter that had already started shaking her body. "Ugh, grow a sense of humor Savior." She turned to me and tugged me inside. "Come on, baby."

Instantly all traces of humor were gone. Savior was a surly bastard on occasion but everything about him vibrated with worry. Anger. Frustration. Maybe even a hint of fear, which meant the shit had hit the fan.

Or it was about to.

"What's up?" I stood between the sofa and loveseat with my arms crossed, waiting for someone to tell me what the hell was going on. "Well?"

Savior sighed and scraped a hand over his face. "Gunnar and Stitch are missing."

"And we're all on lockdown," Teddy added, aggravation rolling off her in waves. She put up with a lot of club shit because the Reckless Bastards were my family, but the seemingly regular lockdowns always made things tense between us. Teddy was a creature of habit and she didn't like her whole world flipped upside down as a precaution. "Again."

Shit. "Okay. What do we know?"

"Apparently we can't leave these guys alone for even a few days without the whole club going to hell."

Lasso's joke produced a few chuckles but Savior's lack of a smile told me exactly how serious this shit was already.

"It's been at least two days as far as we can tell. Jag and Vivi are at the club house doing their digital shit to see what they can find." The words came out robotic, wooden, a testament to just how bothered Savior was.

"Vivi? She's here?" I asked Savior. "She okay?"

"Yeah, she's here and okay. Working her little ass off right now. We need to get going." Savior said. I nodded and turned to Teddy.

"What do you need to grab?"

"Nothing," she said, rolling her eyes and sighing heavily to tell me exactly what she thought of the plan. "We've been there for days already. We just came here to greet you properly."

"Yeah? You waitin' for a kiss too, Savior?"

He grunted and stood. "Nope. I was waiting for that sweet ass." Finally his lips twitched and then a deep laugh spilled from him, startling Quinn at first before she joined in like she was in on the joke. "Lock up. We need to get back to the clubhouse."

Of course we did. Two of our brothers were missing which meant we were on high alert and I only had one other concern. "Where's Max?"

"Keeping an eye on the shop. He said you wouldn't want to close and with those fancy artists there, he wanted to keep an eye on shit in case anyone showed up."

My brother Max was the best damn man I knew. He'd come back from the brink of hell and was as solid as they came. "All right, then let's get going." I gave Teddy one last lingering look. "I guess later'll have to wait."

"Guess so. But you can tell me all about your week when we get settled. Whenever that is." Yeah, she wasn't happy about the situation, but Teddy understood how serious it was so she bit her tongue, which I appreciated.

"I love you."

She smiled. "Of course you do, I'm amazing."

"You love me too, Daddy!" Quinn leapt from Lasso's arms to mine with a big laugh.

"You know I do, Princess." I smacked a kiss to her cheek that had her giggling so hard she nearly fell out of my arms. I grabbed the bag Teddy had packed for me by the door and we all headed out.

Into another goddamn storm.

Chapter Thirteen - Stitch

"How many days do you think we've been in here?" I could hear the shakiness in my voice but it was too damn late to worry about that now. We'd been beaten two times just for fucking sport. Gunnar's hero moves getting us out of the wrist cuffs was a fucking waste of time. As soon as Carlito saw we got free, he had his thugs beat the shit out of us and now they kept us tied up. I swore as soon as we got out of this place, Carlito was a fucking dead man.

"Don't know," Gunnar gasped before spitting out what I could only guess was blood. "Maybe two or three days."

It was hard to tell because one of Carlito's henchmen had put black tape over the windows so we couldn't tell when it was day or night. The thick cement walls made it hard to hear anything so it could have been three days or three weeks for all we knew. "I think that fucker broke a rib."

Gunnar huffed out a bitter laugh. "Take in a deep breath."

"Why?" That sounded like the exact wrong thing to do for broken ribs.

"If it hurts like a motherfucker, your ribs are broken. If they only hurt like a son of a bitch, they're just bruised." With the amusement in his voice I couldn't tell if he was fucking with me or not, but I did it anyway. "Shit that hurts! But they're not broken."

"Good."

Gunnar actually sounded like he meant it, which was hard for me to believe since he'd made no secret out of the fact he thought this was all my fault. Which it was.

"You'll live long enough for me to beat some sense into you."

I huffed out a laugh, not because anything was funny with us both kidnapped, beaten and bloody, but because it was such a damn Gunnar thing to say. "Your compassion is overwhelming, bro."

"I'm compassionate as fuck," he shot back, spitting again. "I'm gonna wait until we're safe and healed first."

Yeah, I suppose that was fair. "What the fuck are we gonna do?" Neither of us could take any more beatings before something broke or ruptured, resulting in our eventual deaths.

Gunnar sighed and I could hear the sound of the wooden chair he was tied to groaning under his massive size. "Find a way out of this fuckin' place, that's what."

The door opened and the lights switched on, temporarily blinding me until the only thing in my vision was the crazy bastard called Guapo. He was at least six feet tall and built like a fucking refrigerator with a long, ugly fucking scar from the left corner of his mouth all the way to his ear. I could only imagine the painful story behind it, but it didn't make me warm up to the fucker. "What the fuck do you want?"

The bastard grinned and it wasn't just basic happiness, no, it was the smile of a man who enjoyed causing pain. "I could beat you until you're just a puddle of meat and blood, but *El Jefe* wants to talk to you."

The sound of Carlito's bitch heels sounded loud on the concrete floor in short, quick steps, getting closer until he reached us.

"I have a proposition for you." He gave us each a death stare and stepped in front of Gunnar. "Between the two of you, you seem to be the smarter man, so let's make a deal." The little fucker laughed like he'd just told the best fucking joke around.

"Ain't exactly a deal with me tied to a fucking chair, is it?" That was Gunnar, tough until the very fucking end, even with ropes wrapped around his wrists.

Carlito threw his head back and laughed. "Well I would be stupid to release you when you have that look on your face. Like you want to kill me, no?"

"I can't say for sure how fucking stupid you are. *Jefe*. What the fuck do you want?"

Instantly his demeanor changed from playful to serious, hands folded in front of him as he kept a respectable distance between himself and Gunnar. "What I want is an exchange. Your lives for…let's call it a *favor*."

"Again, not a fucking *favor* if my life is on the line."

Guapo sent a fist flying right into Gunnar's stomach, but that tough son of a bitch didn't let out so much as a grunt. Carlito barked, "Let him speak!"

"You hit like a bitch." Gunnar spit blood, barely missing Guapo's pointy ass leather shoes. He couldn't help but taunt the stocky fucker.

Guapo leaned in, eager to land another blow but Carlito put up a hand to step in. "Are you ready to listen?"

"My ears ain't taped shut, are they?"

Carlito's brown eyes narrowed but he banked his temper, probably because he realized that was as good as he'd get from Gunnar. "Right. Well I have a shipment here but I need it to be someplace else."

Gunnar scoffed. "Where exactly is here?"

"Come on now. Let's not play games."

Gunnar flicked a look at me that was equal parts frustration and amusement before he switched his gaze back to the little man with the chunky psychopath at his side. "Since I was knocked out when we got here, and we haven't left this fucking room, you're gonna have to tell me, *Jefe*."

Carlito sighed and crossed his arms before uncrossing them self-consciously. "We're in *Mexico*," he conceded. "Now, I need you to get this shipment from this side of the border all the way up to Reno."

"And for this, we get to get the fuck outta here?"

Carlito nodded and Gunnar scoffed. "So much for this being about your bitch."

Then Guapo hit him again, right in the face and it only made Gunnar smile. "Watch your mouth."

"Get this rope off me and then say that." His voice pitched low, lethal even, and Carlito took a step back. Guapo took a step forward but it was a mistake because Gunnar had spent every free second he had loosening the ropes. The crazy fucker had dislocated his thumb last night trying to loosen them enough that he could slip in and out of them with ease. One of his legs was free now, too. Thanks to the rickety ass chair that could barely hold his weight. As soon as Guapo was close enough, Gunnar swept his foot forward, catching the creep until he was on the ground. His head hit with a sickening crack. "Bad move, *Guapo*."

"Get up!" Carlito shouted at his henchman, the panic in his voice bouncing off the walls as he took another step back. And another. And another fucking step.

Pussy.

"I said get up, motherfucker! Get. Up!"

Guapo tried but Gunnar had unleashed the beast, cracking his now free hand against the arm of the chair until the wood snapped and freed his other hand. Then the crazy bastard broke the rest of the chair over Guapo's back until it was in shards all around him. "Yeah, Guapo. Get. The. Fuck. Up!" He roared like a man possessed, urging Guapo to his feet while Carlito yelled in the background.

Carlito moved away, one step at a time, but he was too focused on Gunnar and Guapo to remember me until he tripped over my legs. "You motherfucker!" He scrambled up on all fours before struggling to his feet in those slippery ass bitch heels he wore.

"You'll regret that." He sneered, his eyes narrow and menacing. The fucker was a goddamn contradiction; equal parts terrifyingly cold and scared of his own fucking shadow. "I doubt it." I spat out.

Carlito rushed to the door, pounding on it with his fists and speaking in very fast, panicked Spanish.

When the door opened, he stumbled back and shouted an order to the two armed men who couldn't have been more than twenty or twenty-one years old. "*Rapido!*" He turned his dark, icy glare back to me. "We could have done this the easy way."

"Easy?" Gunnar's question came out as a feral roar as he landed one last sickening blow to Guapo's face, rendering the man unconscious. "The easy way would have involved asking, not fucking kidnapping or attempted fucking murder!"

Carlito scoffed but kept his distance and I couldn't say I blamed him. At all. Right now Gunnar was the more terrifying of the two. "If I wanted you dead, you would be dead."

"Maybe so," Gunnar snapped, "but we ain't dead yet, are we? And now you need something from us so it seems like all your talk about your precious side piece was nothing more than bullshit so you could find two errand boys."

Guapo finally stood with a grunt and Gunnar looked over his shoulder before sending an elbow flying at his nose. He flashed a satisfied smile when the man went down, leaving droplets of blood flying all around.

Carlito shook his head in disgust and turned to me with a malicious grin that twisted his features. "Errand boys, I like the sound of that. Particularly because I have something you want."

Gunnar barked out a laugh. "I can assure you that you don't have shit I want."

Carlito's lips curled up and a chill went through me. "Maybe not you, but your friend and I seem to have the same taste in women." He snapped his fingers twice and one of the armed men appeared with a hand squeezing Marisol's arm tight enough to make her cry out. I struggled not to go after the bastard for pushing her to the ground. "Ah yes, I thought this might get your attention." He grabbed that same arm and yanked Marisol to her feet.

"She has nothing to do with me," Gunnar spat out, glaring at me and daring me to disagree. I knew I shouldn't, that choosing her could mean war with a fucking cartel but looking at her, bruised and bloody and shaken, how could I leave her to that fate? I wasn't that fucking cold.

"It would seem that your friend would disagree." Carlito seemed way too pleased with himself, until six feet six inches of angry Gunnar in all his baldheaded glory stalked his way, then he took a step back.

"Then that's between you and him. It's got fuck all to do with me." A sliver of unease ran through me at how fast Gunnar was walking. He was either deadly fucking serious or on a suicide mission and considering he had his baby sister to think about, the only option was *deadly fucking serious*.

Carlito shouted, "Stop him!"

One of the armed men stepped into Gunnar's path but before he could aim his M4 Carbine, Gunnar had the man pressed against the wall, his feet dangling about three inches from the ground with nothing but his own gun at his throat to keep him from falling.

"Yeah, stop me." Gunnar's voice was low and menacing but his movements were calm. Calculated.

Gunnar meant business but so did Carlito if Marisol's swollen eye had anything to do with it. He gripped her hair and pulled hard enough that she fell to her knees in pain.

"Gunnar!" I shouted.

He wasn't listening, goddammit. "Gunnar," I yelled again but he was someplace else. In the dark place a man had to go when he had to take a life. It was never easy, definitely not for soldiers who had to kill people who didn't look like they expected you to. But we weren't at war. Not yet. "Goddammit Gunnar, stop it!"

He pulled back the gun, letting the man drop to his knees before he sent a size thirteen boot crashing down on his cheek. Then he turned to me, rage burning in his blue eyes. "What the fuck?"

My gaze slid to Marisol who trembled with fear. Her brown skin was tear-streaked and dirty, her hair matted like she'd been in another dark room for as long as we had. Gunnar nodded reluctantly and aimed the gun at the ground. It was the only fucking sign I would get.

"What's in the truck?" I asked Carlito.

He looked at me with fire in his eyes. "That's not your business."

"Bullshit," I spat at him, feeling helpless still strapped to the fucking chair. I let my gaze fall on Marisol who looked resigned to her fate and I knew then that it didn't matter what was inside.

Carlito laughed triumphantly. "I thought you would see things my way."

"He might but I don't." Gunnar took a step closer, slowly lifting the gun until it was trained on Carlito. "What's in the goddamn truck?"

The bastard gripped her hair tighter and Marisol released another tortured cry. "I could break her beautiful neck right now."

Gunnar shrugged, finger slowly moving to the trigger like it would mean nothing to him to kill Carlito. "She doesn't mean shit to me, Carlito. But I was trained by the good ol' U.S. government which means I could kill you and all of your men before they even get their finger on the trigger. So, go on, test me."

Marisol looked at me, fear shining in her eyes and making her body shudder, pleading with me to help. She squeezed her brown eyes shut and clenched her jaws against the pain of Carlito's tight grip. "Please," she mouthed to me.

Carlito loosened his grip but not before yanking Marisol back to her feet. "Fine. Maybe a few more days will make you more agreeable." He grinned but it looked more like a grimace, showing off teeth that looked like they'd been bleached so many times they might crumble at the slightest pressure. "You can handle a few more days, can't you Marisol?"

She kept her eyes closed and said nothing, but she didn't have to because I knew. Whatever he'd put me and Gunnar through over the past few days was nothing compared to what he'd done to her.

"*Contestame!!*"

She nodded but her eyes never opened and her body shook even harder. "Yes," she squeaked out.

"Good. Because until you agree, she will get enough punishment for three." The room fell silent beyond Marisol's sniffles and Gunnar and I both heard the telltale click of a gun.

He turned a half a second before I did, squeezing the trigger three times until the other armed guard was nothing more than a memory. Then he turned to the other guard he'd choked earlier and put one round in his leg before he faced Carlito. "Or I could just put a bullet in you now and all three of us just walk out of here. What's it gonna be, *Jefe*?"

Carlito swallowed hard at the lethal look on Gunnar's face, slowly moving Marisol between them but he miscalculated because Gunnar didn't let the gun fall, not one fucking millimeter. "You would kill me over a woman?"

"Hell no. I'll kill you for plenty of reasons but never for a chick. But," he raised the gun over Marisol's head so it was trained right on Carlito's forehead. "If it makes you feel any better, we can say it's because of her."

"Or," Carlito added with a nervous grin. "I could pay you for your trouble and if you complete the job, I'll return Marisol to your friend. And," he added nervously when Gunnar adjusted his grip on the firearm, "no further harm will come to her."

Gunnar dropped the barrel with an annoyed sigh. "If she's not in Reno when we get there *and* unharmed, I'll blow up the fucking shipment no matter *what* it is. And I'll kill everyone in sight."

Carlito grinned, impressed. "It's too bad we met the way we did, I could use someone of your caliber." Gunnar grunted but I didn't miss the angry glare Carlito slanted at Guapo, coming to on the ground. "Good help is impossible to find."

Marisol's brown eyes met mine and I gave her a quick wink before Carlito pulled her away. Despite his rough treatment, I relaxed because I knew something Marisol didn't. He cared more about his shipment than he did about her. She was worth nothing to him in comparison to whatever was in that fucking truck.

When the door closed, Gunnar growled. "You're dead fucking meat, kid. Dead fucking meat."

I did the only thing I could in the situation. I grinned.

Chapter Fourteen - Jag

After spending the past four days digging into Reed Henderson's background, his life and every fucking person he'd ever crossed paths with, I'd come up with nothing. "Not one goddamn thing," I said to no one in particular, even though Vivi sat less than five feet away from me with her pretzels, diet root beer and fingers flying over the keyboard.

"Poor baby," she said with her trademark snark and a sexy little smirk on her face while she continued digging into...*something*. "Guess you better stick to ink."

"Yeah?" I poked her in the side and she laughed, smacking my hand away. "What did you find?"

"Plenty," she said with the same confidence she always had when it came to digging through people's digital footprints. "And in a few minutes I'll wow you with my cyber prowess."

"I'd rather you wow me with something else," I told her and pushed my laptop away, scooting closer to inhale her sexy, tough girl scent. To press my lips to the delicate skin of her neck because every minute I wasn't touching her was a minute wasted. We'd been apart for too long.

"Let me finish this and I'll show you all of my prowess*es*." She laughed and shook her head. "Or whatever the plural of prowess is, I'm gonna show you all of them. Big time."

A deep laugh bubbled out of me at her weird string of word salad, but I wasn't deterred, not when there was all this delicious skin for me to taste. "Then make it snappy, woman."

"Hey, this kind of genius takes time." She stuffed a pretzel in her mouth. "Besides, I prefer to be thorough and believe me, the suits I worked with, they love redundant levels of thorough."

She hadn't said much about her time back on the east coast and if I had to guess I'd say it was deliberate. What I didn't know was if it was because she couldn't talk about it or because there was some underlying issue between us. "Okay, all done." She turned and pressed a kiss to my nose. "Want me to tell you and you can pass the info on, or do a whole presentation for your bros?"

I snickered. "My bros?" She nodded and it made me laugh even harder. "You can tell the bros."

"Great. Gather up the bros, then!" She smiled at me, her gray eyes soft and so filled with love I couldn't help but lean forward to capture her lips in a slow, sensual kiss that probably wasn't the best idea considering how packed the clubhouse was these days.

"Have I told you how glad I am that you're back?"

Vivi smiled against my lips and nodded. "Maybe a time or two. Good thing it never gets old to hear." She pulled my bottom lip between her teeth and tugged gently. "I'm glad to be back. I missed the hell out of you."

"No need to miss me anymore, babe."

"Damn straight. And if we can get this little presentation on the road, I could show you my other prowess-*es*," she said on a snicker, giving me a gentle shove.

I was already on my feet in search of Cross. I found him and Moon getting hot and heavy in his office. "Vivi's found some info she thinks we need to hear."

He groaned but Moon only smiled, giving him one final kiss before pulling back and smoothing her hair. "Hey Jag."

"Lookin' good, Moon."

"You too," she laughed. "Being in love agrees with you."

I smiled and whispered a quick, "Thanks," as she breezed out of the office. Moon seemed a little too hippie dippy at first, but the truth was she was as solid as they came with her good advice, spirituality and keen insights. "So, where do you want to do this?" We didn't allow women or non-members in the Merry

Mayhem room, and this wasn't information for everybody's ears.

"We'll clear out the main room for a while and let the prospects keep an eye on the women and children." Cross stood and raked a hand through his hair, blowing out a deep breath. "Tell me it's good news."

"I don't know, man. I didn't find anything on Reed. Other than a few protests against wars and animal testing and drug laws, the dude is ridiculously clean."

"Shit." Cross grimaced and let out another frustrated breath.

"I know what you mean. Come on. No point in worrying until we have a reason to. Right?"

"Yeah I guess," he grumbled and followed me back into the main room which we cleared out in under three minutes *and* with minimal protests. When everyone was gathered, Cross turned to my girl with a grin. "Okay, Vivi. What did you find?"

She smiled and let out a deep breath, swiping a hand over a mass of messy pink curls. "A lot, actually. First, Marisol. I found two in Reno but one of them is a fifty year old widow. The other one, Marisol Luna, is twenty-six years old and lives in an apartment paid for by Carlito Esteban." She blew out a breath and looked around the room. "I guess none of you have ever heard of him?"

Everyone, including me shook their heads and she nodded. "Okay. Well Carlito Esteban is the head of the Salinas Cartel and has been for the past fifteen years. His uncle, Cadre, sat at the top of the cartel for more than three decades before dying in a mysterious accident, which is widely believed to be caused by Carlito, who was just sixteen at the time."

Savior let out a low whistle. "Fuck."

"Shit, Stitch never does trouble halfway, does he?" Lasso's words added levity to the atmosphere but he wasn't wrong. Not this time, anyway.

"That's not all," Vivi said, her voice growing wary. "Since Carlito took over, Salinas has become one of the deadliest cartels on the planet thanks to *pequeño diablo*, which is what the Mexican papers call him. Little Devil. They peddle in drugs including pot, heroin and their biggest money maker, synthetic drugs, but they also do well in human trafficking and illegal gun sales, with earnings estimated by the FBI to be in excess of a billion dollars."

Cross smacked one hand against the metal table, his anger palpable. "Why the fuck don't we know this guy?"

"'Cause we don't fuck with the cartels, man," I answered back.

Cross asked, "So what are we up against, Vivi?"

"Truth? A big ol' fuck fest. These guys aren't just deadly, they're reckless. Last year they were responsible—reportedly—for more than fifteen hundred murders."

"Fuck. How in the hell are we supposed to find them?" Cross's frustration was building by the second but Vivi, to her credit didn't look bothered. At all.

"Well the good news, if you can call it that, is that I have photos of *El Jefe* and his number two, Guapo, who acts as one of the Salinas enforcers. If Carlito is up here in the states, I'd be surprised."

She picked up her laptop and squinted at the screen from about three inches away, frowning at whatever held her attention. "It looks like they might be related but I won't be able to tell until I have a specialist take a look at these documents."

Mexico was notorious for their shoddy recordkeeping so I could only imagine what she was staring at.

"I'll keep digging for confirmation on that, but I do have Marisol's address."

"Thank fuck for that," Cross mumbled, pulling out his buzzing phone and frowning at the screen. "Thanks, Vivi."

He was distracted and spoke quickly and quietly into the phone before turning back to us.

She nodded and took the hint, grabbing her laptop before doing a sexy little finger wave to the crowd. "No problem. Good luck, bros." Then she was gone and Cross stood in her place, a dark scowl on his face.

"I wish your girl could've given us better news, Jag." Cross let out a harsh laugh and shook his head. "But at least now we know what we're up against. Savior and I will ride up to Reno, see what we can find from this Marisol chick." He issued the rest of his orders, which mostly consisted of sticking close to the clubhouse and making sure all the women and children were accounted for. Regularly.

As soon as the meeting broke up, I strode out of the clubhouse and across the parking lot to Vivi's camper. I opened the door and listened for movement but there was none so I stepped inside and called out. "Hey Vivi, have I told you how sexy it is when you get all tech nerd on me?" She was smart as hell, confident in her skills and most of all, my girl had no qualms about showing me how she felt.

"Not in the past five minutes," she called out from the bedroom. "Come closer and tell me again."

I heard the laughter in her voice and made my way to the back of the camper, stopping in the doorway at the sight of my woman stretched out on the bed, wrapped up in black lace that showed off more than it covered. Not that I was complaining. "Fuck, babe. You look good enough to eat."

She licked her lips like I was her favorite meal as her breath hitched at my words, her gaze was black with desire. Arousal. "Then eat me." Vivi's legs fell open, the tiny strip of fabric barely covering the pussy lips I couldn't wait to put my mouth on.

Her fingers slid between her legs and my grin widened as my cock turned to steel. My girl was a lot of things, but she was about as subtle as a sledgehammer. "You want me to taste you, Vivi?"

She shook her head and propped her body up on her elbows. "No Jag, I want you to devour me."

HOLIDAY HAVOC

With those words, how could I do anything else? My shirt came off and went straight to the floor as I leaned forward, half my body hanging off the bed. My shoulders kept her legs open but I palmed her thighs and widened her even more so I could look. Stare. Watch as that pretty pink pussy pulsed for me, glistening and swollen because she wanted me so fucking bad. "Damn you got such a pretty pussy." She pulsed again at my words and I growled a half a second before I put my mouth on her, licking and sucking her until she whimpered.

My Vivi, fucking whimpering with need. Grinding against my face as she arched into me. She was slick and sweet, legs wrapped around me tight like she was afraid I might get up and walk away, as if I ever would. Not when she let out those husky cries and urged me to lick her harder, to suck her clit. "Fuck me with your tongue, Jag."

My dirty fucking girl. I loved it when she talked dirty and I gave her exactly what she wanted, nearly coming in my pants at the way she held my head and looked at me while my tongue disappeared inside her creamy cunt. I moaned against her and she trembled and then vibrated against me.

So fucking close.

With a smack of her ass, I flipped us so she was on top, pussy flush against my lips while her clit nudged my nose with every swirl of her hips. "Oh fuck, Jag. Yes!" She didn't just grind against me, she fucked my face, back and forth she slid against me, up and down until her walls pulsed on my tongue. "Yes! Oh!" I surprised her, slipping my middle finger between her fine ass cheeks and into that tight little rosette. "Shit, yeah! Jag," she cried out as her orgasm started in her toes but her body never stopped moving, never stopped chasing her pleasure.

She was close, bucking against me but unable to get away. A move forward and she was impaled on my tongue, a move back and my finger slid deeper into her ass. It was too many sensations and I was sure I would come right along with her. Then Vivi froze and slid down my body, hands moving frantically to open my pants and tug them down and as soon as they were, she was there, sliding down the length of my cock until her tight, hot pussy engulfed me. "Oh, fuck."

"Jag," she grunted as her body shook violently with pleasure, squeezing the fuck out of me and pulling the fastest orgasm ever out of me. "Damn, I love you."

"Love you more," I grunted as she continued to pulse around me, shivering with the aftershocks of pleasure. When her tongue licked up the side of my neck and ended with her teeth sinking into my earlobe, I was ready to go again.

Forever.

KB WINTERS

Chapter Fifteen – Cross

The ride up to Reno was quiet and somber, Savior was content to keep a respectable distance between us with minimal conversation. Both of us were too lost in our own thoughts to do anything more than enjoy the scenery and hope like hell our brothers were still breathing. We'd left just before dawn and beat most of the traffic, arriving a little after noon to the address Vivi had given us.

"So this is it, huh? Looks like a fucking roach motel." Savior's words mirrored my own thoughts as we stood in front of a shitty little apartment complex that looked like it used to be a roadside motel.

"This is the address Vivi sent to my phone." And even if I thought she was a little strange, I knew she was a genius when it came to hacking into shit that people didn't want found. The fact that Carlito owned the building had been buried behind layers of shell corporations, and probably meant he didn't want anyone to know about her, either. "How in the fuck did Stitch get mixed up with a cartel mistress in the fucking ghetto"

Savior let out a bitter laugh, shaking his head because he didn't have any answers either. "Fuck if I know. I wanted to believe Reed was involved because the coincidence is too strong, but it had to be dumb fucking luck. He probably met her on all those trips up here to set up the deal with Reed."

"Yeah, that's what I was thinking too." It would've been easier if Reed was involved but Jag had done more than enough digging and found nothing. Less than fucking nothing. I let out a long breath and looked at the cement steps, stained with gum, graffiti and piss. This was a place people went when they had nothing else to do. Nowhere else to go. "He's got all that money and he keeps his girl here?" This place wouldn't see repairs unless they were absolutely necessary.

Savior shrugged his shoulders and dropped them with a weary sigh. "We going up or do we need hazmat suits first?"

HOLIDAY HAVOC

"We're going up." There was no point in delaying the inevitable, but the lack of police cars and yellow tape gave me hope.

"Lead the way, Prez." His tone sounded about as hopeful as I felt which is to say, not very.

The painted green doors were chipped all over and, in some places, a number or two was missing and hadn't been replaced. "This place is a fucking dump." But we were here now and we needed to find Stitch and Gunnar so I put my hand on the door and Savior stopped me. "What?"

"Be careful." He nodded in the direction of the door, closed but the shitty lock gave way with a flick of his hand.

"Fuck!" I pushed it open without thinking and froze at the sight of the shitty little apartment. "What the fuck?" The blue-gray carpet looked as though it hadn't been cleaned since the seventies and the cheap coffee table was broken in shards, like someone had fallen on it. Or been thrown.

"Something went down here."

"Yeah, looks like it." He was right but as I looked around at all the evidence of the struggle that had taken place here, my hope began to fade. A large pool of blood was already dry in one corner of the living room. Too much blood to belong to someone who was still breathing. "Shit. I hope to God that blood doesn't belong to one of ours."

Savior nodded grimly and bent down behind the sofa. "Check this out." He rose with a bloody knife in his hand. A familiar blade with a gold and pearl handle, given to Gunnar by his old man before he split. He carried that damn thing with him everywhere, from the small blue collar town he grew up in to the deserts of the Middle East and back. "At least we know they were here."

"You think this was a setup?" It didn't make any fucking sense. A guy with billions of dollars putting his side piece up in this shithole.

"Maybe. I don't know." Savior didn't elaborate and I didn't need him to because it didn't matter. He'd heard the same info I did from Vivi's mouth and knew this Carlito asshole was dangerous and crazy, a lethal combination for sure.

"We need to figure out where they are first and then what the fuck this asshole wants, because if he wanted them dead, I figure we'd have found their bodies already." It was a gruesome thought but one I hadn't stopped thinking about since I got Reed's call.

"Fuck," Savior sighed. "You're right."

"I know Vivi and Jag are on this but I'm gonna talk to Dodds."

"The cop?" Savior said it like the man hadn't saved Moon from his crooked partner which I could never forget. "You must be more worried than you look."

"Goddamn right I am. Did you not hear the deadliest cartel on the planet part of what Vivi said? Because I can't stop thinking about it. And they've got my men." I let out a long breath. I knew Dodds was just doing his job but that didn't mean I wasn't appreciative. "Dodds has to have some information that could be useful."

Skepticism was written all over Savior's face but I didn't give a damn. If the Salinas Cartel had Gunnar and Stitch, I'd use all the resources at my disposal. I would fucking destroy them. "So who called to put that frown on your face?"

"Gabe, Prez for Sons of Sin MC. I reached out to see if they had any dealings with Salinas."

"And? Don't leave me in fucking suspense, man." Savior continued looking around the tiny shitty apartment.

"And all he had to say was he'd gone up against a few lackeys in the Salinas Cartel when they were trying to find Ripcord's sister and lost a few brothers before it was all over. Long story short, these guys are bad fucking news."

Savior sighed, the sound was as exhausted as I felt. "Fuck man, I was really hoping for a holiday filled with peace and quiet, Mandy's sweet treats and her sexy little body."

"Yeah, no fucking kidding." I'd hoped for a quiet holiday with Moon and Beau, but this was our life. Chaos and death and imminent fucking war at all times.

We finished looking around the little apartment, noting that Marisol was nowhere to be found but the closet and drawers were still filled with her clothes, shoes and toiletries. Everything said she'd planned to come back at some point. *If* she left of her own free will. "Stay here a few hours and see if she returns."

He nodded even though he was unhappy with the assignment. "And what are you gonna do?"

"Talk to Dodds and then see if Vivi and Jag came up with anything else we could use." I didn't know shit about the cartel up here in Reno, but I would reach out to every fucking person I knew to find out more. "Wait a few hours and if she doesn't show, get back to Mayhem."

"Be careful and don't tell that cop too much."

"Thanks, man." We both walked back to the parking lot. I got on my bike while Savior moved his to a spot in the back so he could watch the apartment without being seen. "Later."

I hauled ass on the seven-hour ride home, eager to hook up with Dodds. When I was close to Mayhem, I pulled over to a gas station and gave him a call before it got too late. Asked him to meet me somewhere away from prying eyes. Forty minutes later he pulled up in his unmarked burgundy Crown Vic and parked beside my bike. I chose a spot at the east end of town away from all the shops and restaurants just to make sure we could speak in private. "Detective."

His lips tightened into a smile at the greeting and he nodded. "Cross. What can I do for you?"

"Max said you came in asking questions about a cartel. Did you have a specific one in mind or were you just fishing?"

His posture went stiff and I knew he would go on the defensive because, well, cops. "I already told Max I wasn't trying to jam you up."

I sighed and took a deep breath. "I didn't come here to fight, Dodds. I just want some information. Did you have a specific cartel in mind?" He shook his head and I felt a little more hope fade away. "Gunnar and Stitch are missing and we have reason to believe the Salinas Cartel has him."

Dodds whistled, his eyes wide with disbelief. "How did you get mixed up with those guys? They're crazy as hell."

"We didn't," I admitted with a frustrated groan. "As far as I can tell, this started over a woman."

Dodds barked out a laugh. "Isn't it always over a woman?" He shook his head again and scrubbed a hand down his face, looking every inch like the overworked law enforcement officer he was. "Salinas don't fuck around Cross. They kidnap kids and sell them to the highest bidder. Adoptions, sex trade or worse. The ones they can't sell, they turn them out and put them on the streets of cities around Mexico and the U.S. until they overdose or get killed."

"That's basically what my source said, too." Only with a lot less detail which I made a note to myself to thank Vivi for later. "But that's not their bread and butter, right?"

"Hell no. Drugs. Pot used to be their cash cow but with all the border states but Texas legalizing it, they diversified." He said the last word with a snort. "Heroin is always a good money maker, but the South American cartels have that sewn up pretty tight. So they started manufacturing and selling synthetic drugs. Ecstasy, speed, Oxy. A lot of money and a lot of deaths, both from drug overdose and murder."

"Shit." Vivi had definitely sanitized the picture for our benefit and while I appreciated it, now I couldn't stop thinking about what my guys were going through. "Do you know where they operate out of?"

"Mexico mostly but I suspect they have connections in more than a few American cities." He eyed me carefully, weighing if I was about to do something really fucking stupid that would make his life harder. "What are you planning?"

I pulled the lone cigarette I kept on me since I quit from behind my ear and lit it, inhaling deeply, ignoring the pang of conscience at what Moon would say when she inevitably smelled it on me. I'd worry about that later though because this little stick of nicotine was the only thing keeping me sane in the moment. "You know the answer to that. I'll do what I have to do to get my guys back."

He nodded, unhappy about my words but resigned to my decision. "Be careful, Cross. Salinas combines all the worst of the groups. They rape for punishment, kill for sport and do it in the most gruesome ways possible. Look up what happened to the former Mayor of Mexico City."

"I will, and thanks Dodds."

"No problem." I turned to my bike, thinking that was another fucking thing to come at the club. I was sure after the shit that went down last year with

Detective Haynes and Pacheco that we'd have a year or two of goddamn peace. "Hey Cross?"

"Yeah?" I looked back over my shoulder.

"Call me when you need me. I'll offer whatever help I can."

"Thanks, Dodds. You're all right."

"Thanks," he snorted. "Tell that to my precinct."

I could only imagine what it was like for him, the guy who took down a dirty cop, in a building full of cops who strongly believed in the thin blue fucking line. "Fuck' em. You're a good man, Dodds."

He nodded and I hopped on my bike, eager to get back home and see my woman and my kid.

Chapter Sixteen - Stitch

I didn't know how many days had passed since we made the devil's deal with Carlito, but it felt like weeks since I'd last been in my bed. My apartment. With my club. Hell, I hadn't seen or heard one peep from Marisol since Gunnar killed one of Carlito's men and laid Guapo out. "How long do you think it's been, Gunnar?"

"At least a week, maybe more. Why the hell you so concerned with how long we've been here? You should be more worried about when we're getting the fuck out. If we're getting the fuck out."

As usual, he was a grouchy fucker only this time I couldn't blame him. We hadn't had much to eat since we got here because Gunnar was sure Carlito was trying to poison us.

I didn't believe it, but I wasn't dumb enough to risk it. No matter what Gunnar thought. "I'm just fucking curious, man."

"Sorry," he grunted out. "We have to do something, Stitch. If I stay here another day, I'll lose my shit and murder everyone."

"Say the word," I laughed, "and I'll be your partner in crime."

"Always, kid." He flashed a smile in my direction and I didn't know if that smile was Gunnar being nice because he thought we were about to die or because he actually didn't hate me the way he seemed to all the damn time.

Carlito had made Guapo lock the door after Gunnar had gone all Rambo on their asses. The big metal door made a lot of fucking noise when it was being disengaged. It would be impossible to sneak in with that loud thing announcing their arrival, which meant it was the only reason either of us had gotten any sleep since we got here.

"Good morning!" Carlito's chipper voice sounded, honest to fucking God, like nails on a chalkboard and the only reason I hadn't brained the fucker was because of Marisol. "I hope you slept well."

HOLIDAY HAVOC

"A bed would've been real fucking nice," Gunnar grunted out, refusing to do anything that might make Carlito think he had the upper fucking hand.

"Yes, I'm sure it would be," he said with a giant fucking smirk that a man wore when he got laid and that thought only pissed me off. It made me see red. It made me want to get up on my feet and pound that fucker's face until he was completely unrecognizable. "Smile boys, today is a good day!"

That false chipper shit grated on my nerves, but I kept quiet because he seemed to want to piss me off. Probably because he couldn't stand the thought of another man being inside Marisol.

"What's so good about it?" Gunnar rose to his full height and squared his wide shoulders, intimidating even when he wasn't trying to be. Carlito took an unconscious step back.

With a snap of his fingers, Carlito produced Marisol who looked frail and pale. Based on the colors of her fading bruises it looked like pequeño diablo had kept his word. "I thought you might like to say goodbye to Marisol since you're leaving today."

I didn't trust this fucker. "What's the catch?"

"No catch," he said quickly but his lips twitched and there was a gleam in his eyes that I didn't like.

Gunnar took a step forward, anger emanating off him but I saw the smile in his eyes when Carlito slid Marisol between them. *Fuckin' pussy.* "You mean see you soon, right?" Arms crossed to show off twenty-one inch biceps, Gunnar took another step forward at Carlito's confused expression. "You said *goodbye* but that would indicate we wouldn't see her again. So you meant to say *see you soon*, didn't you?"

He swallowed, eyes wide with fear and trying hard not to show it. For the boss of a huge cartel, he sure was wimpy. But whatever this place was, it wasn't his main base of operations because he didn't replace the man Gunnar killed and the other one was still walking with a limp from the bullet that went through his leg. "Of course. Just a slip of the tongue."

"Fine. What time do we leave?" Gunnar barked the question at him, his tone said he wasn't in the mood for a bullshit answer.

"Soon." That was all Carlito said and Gunnar nodded, drawing a smile from the tiny fucker.

"Good. Leave her with us until we go." Carlito sucked in a breath, ready to argue but Gunnar held up a hand. "We just want to make sure she's all right. Unless you're planning to back out of our deal?"

"No, of course not." Carlito shook his head a little too quickly and Gunnar noticed it too but stood still as a stone. His face emotionless. Blank and scary as hell. "She can stay but don't think of doing anything to her."

Gunnar scoffed and arched a brow. "That's your style, not mine."

"*Jefe.*" Guapo stood in the doorway glaring at Gunnar with a gun in his hands as he waited for Carlito to answer.

"What?" he snapped and whirled around on those fancy boots with the heels on them.

"It's time to get the truck loaded."

Carlito nodded and turned back to Gunnar. "Fine, you can keep her for now. I'll be back."

"Don't fuck with me, Carlito."

"Watch your fuckin' mouth," Guapo snapped at him and Gunnar smiled.

"Ready for ass kicking number two, fat boy?" Angry, Guapo took a step before but that was it before Carlito put a hand to his chest.

"We don't have time for this. Go load the truck and I'll come check on it. Now." He turned again with a smile. "Remember who she belongs to."

When the door locked, Gunnar groaned. "Are you really fucking that guy because I'm getting strong feminine vibes from him."

Marisol still shook with fear but her lips twitched. "You don't have to do this," she said, her voice so damn small that if I wasn't looking I wouldn't believe it was her.

"I know I don't, sweetheart. But I also don't let innocent women get caught up in shit they don't deserve." His gaze hardened. "You don't deserve this, do you?"

She sighed and her legs wobbled, sending me up on my feet and charging towards her, but Gunnar was closer and he scooped her in his arms first and set her on the chair he'd been sitting in. "Thanks. No, I don't deserve it. At least I don't think so."

"Of course you don't Marisol, don't even think that shit. Fuck that guy," I told her and wrapped my arms around her. When she closed her eyes and leaned into me, I noticed her soft curves had faded a little. She'd lost some weight and that just pissed me off. "Are you okay?" I cupped her cheeks and looked deep into big coffee brown eyes that had lost their spark. Seeing those dark brown eyes with ribbons of caramel and amber in them without their signature spark pissed me off and I knew I'd find a way to kill that asshole.

"A little sore but I'll be fine, Stitch. Don't worry about me." She looked from me to Gunnar and back to me with a sigh. "You can't trust Carlito," she whispered. "He won't keep his word, not about anything. Ever."

"Don't worry about us," Gunnar told her and crouched down in front of her. "Tell me the truth, did that asshole keep his word about hurting you?"

Marisol stared at Gunnar for a long time, brown eyes taking in every detail to see if he was someone she could trust. Not that I blamed her, his words were firm and not even a little fucking nice so she had a right to question him. "He didn't touch me. Kept me in the room next door. Alone except when someone brought food."

"Good. That means he gives a shit about whatever this shipment is. Sorry to tell you, but he cares more about that shipment than you."

"Gunnar, what the fuck man?"

He shrugged. "She needs to know the goddamn truth, Stitch. To make sure she's not holding out hope that he'll leave his wife and kids for her. That she's not thinking about double-crossing us when we get to the other side." He was talking to me, but Gunnar's blue eyes were glued to hers, taking in every detail, every muscle twitch and every time her eyes moved. "Well?"

"I already know that," she sighed with exhaustion. But her shoulders squared, showing signs that she was coming back to life. "I don't love him, but whatever you think of me, I'm stuck with him. Every time I've tried to leave, he would sabotage my job. My apartment. My friends." Her hands fisted around the hem of her shirt, eyes focused on some faraway time in the past. "I didn't know he was married at first and by the time I found out, there was no fucking leaving."

Gunnar placed one big hand over hers, the other stroking his beard, which by now was in need of a thorough washing. "I'm not judging you, honey."

She snorted. "I may be a mistress, but I am not an idiot. And I do hear and comprehend English."

"Jesus. What do you want me to do, tell him I'm willing to die to protect you? That's not how you bargain Marisol, or didn't you learn that at accounting college?"

"You really are a grouchy bastard."

Gunnar barked out a laugh and looked up at me. "So you told her about us but you didn't tell anyone about her?" He shook his head like I was some precocious fucking kid who needed the guiding hand of an adult and I wanted to smack him. "If you had, maybe we'd have gotten some help by now."

"Help? We don't even know where the fuck we are other than Mexico, which is a big fucking country Gunnar!"

He smiled at Marisol. "He gets worked up so easy. Must be love." Before I could say another word, Gunnar stood and moved away. "Have your talk but if I hear anything interesting, I'm lettin' you know now that I will be watching."

I wanted to smash his face for that last comment but the sweet sound of Marisol's laugh stole my attention. Robbed me of my focus and when she smiled, heat bloomed inside of me. "Don't mind Gunnar, he hasn't had a decent meal in however long we've been here."

"It's been awhile, maybe two weeks." She paused to let her words sink in and she sighed. "I had a TV in there and even though its all in Spanish, we're close enough to the border that a few American news stations came through."

"Shit. I thought it had been a few days not a couple weeks." I bet Cross and the rest of the MC were worried as fuck. Like Gunnar said, because no one knew about her, they wouldn't even know where to start looking for us. "Sorry about the mess at your apartment."

"It's not mine."

"I know you're scared, but we got this, Marisol. I got you. Gunnar is a man of his word and he wouldn't leave you to that fucking psycho. Trust me."

She shook her head, leaning her face against my palm. The sight of her bruises, pale green and yellow, made it hard to keep my composure at the thought of the pain she must've gone through. The horror she'd had to endure at the hands of man she had, at one time, had feelings for. "Things are never that easy with Carlito." She was worried about me as much as herself.

"Don't worry babe, we specialize in shit that ain't easy. Next time I see you will be in Reno."

She smiled and leaned further into my hand, pressing a kiss to my palm. "Thank you, Stitch. But really, don't mess around with Carlito on my behalf. He'll never let me go."

I pressed my forehead to hers and inhaled deeply because I knew my words would put hurt in her eyes and that was the last damn thing I wanted to do. "He will, Marisol. He will because Gunnar is right. Whatever he needs us to get to Reno is important to him, that's why he hasn't killed any of us. Enough that he doesn't want to use his regular channels to make it happen. It means he can't afford for Gunnar to make good on his threat. More important to him than you."

She sucked in a breath. A gasp of surprise I assumed but a slow smile crept across her tear-stained face. "God, I hope you're right."

The sound of the lock tore through the relative silence in the room and I took my chance, pressing a hard kiss to her lips before Carlito appeared. Her lips were salty but there was still that hint of cinnamon and sugar and spice that was unmistakably Marisol. "I'll be seeing you again real soon, pretty girl. Just let me get this bullshit handled and I'll be there."

"If not, I get it Stitch. Really." I could see in her eyes that she did. That she expected this would be the last time we'd ever lay eyes on each other.

I knew then that I had to prove her wrong. "See you soon. And when I do, I expect a big sloppy kiss. On my cock."

Her laughter rang out, making Carlito frown. "Time to go boys. I hope you've enjoyed your goodbye?" One dark brow arched in question but all three of us stared at him blankly. "Right well, off you go."

I sent Marisol one last, longing glance and I hoped that nothing would happen that would make a liar out of me. I would get her away from Carlito, no matter what.

I just hoped to have the backing of my MC if it came to that.

Gunnar looked to Marisol with a wink. "See you soon." He pulled her into a hug and whispered something to her I couldn't hear. Normally it would have pissed me off but I knew he wasn't trying to steal my girl, even though she wasn't technically mine. But dammit, I wanted to know what he'd said that made her shoulders sag with relief. Hell, who the fuck was I kidding? I wanted to be the man to say the words that righted her world.

Next time, I promised myself.

"Go before I change my mind!" Carlito's voice grew deep with anger, the phony heavily accented thing he did was nowhere to be heard. "Now," he urged.

"So much for good ol' Mexican hospitality," Gunnar said as he walked by, shoulder checking that bastard hard as he followed Guapo and another man out the door that had held us captive for weeks. Fucking weeks.

Following Gunnar out, I looked around as we turned through several dark corridors and noting all the paintings of alleged saints and so-called Gods and

I knew where we were. A church. Specifically the basement of a church. "A fucking church," I mumbled, drawing the attention of Guapo and the other man.

"Watch your mouth," he spat out with a dark frown, his finger itching to touch the trigger.

Gunnar barked out a laugh as we climbed a narrow, dark staircase. "Beating the fuck out of a woman and two men is allowed inside these *hallowed* fucking walls, but not coarse language? Fucking idiot."

The sunlight hit us both hard, nearly sending me to my knees under the force of her shine. "Fuck me, it's bright out." I could barely keep my eyes open and I had to stop to shield my eyes even as the others kept moving forward. Looking around I noticed the church was run down but the marquee looked updated and cared for.

"Let's go, Stitch!"

I blinked and turned to where Gunnar stood, arms crossed with a frown on his face. "Right." I cast the church one last look before jogging to catch up. "Where's our ride?"

Guapo smirked. "No ride. I have your wallets," he handed one to each of us and kept talking. "The border is an hour's walk that way. Your phones are broken, so I suggest you start walking. It's a long way to El Paso."

I didn't know much about the geography of Texas, but I knew enough to know it was a border town. "El Paso?"

Guapo nodded, his sleazy fucking smirk growing bigger by the second. "That's where you'll relieve the driver. El Paso."

"You motherfucker," Gunnar growled, his voice low and menacing. "If I see you again, I'm gonna rip your fucking brain out through your nose."

Guapo's laughter sounded behind us but neither of us looked back or acknowledged the bastard. We had a long damn walk ahead of us, to the border and then cross over to fucking El Paso. "You got any cash?"

Gunnar sighed and pulled out his wallet. "You lookin' to get some pussy before crossing the border?"

"No, asshole. We need to blend in which means we need a backpack, regular clothes and some goddamn sunglasses."

He flashed a smile at me. "We're gonna make a true Reckless Bastard out of you yet, kid."

Chapter Seventeen - Max

"Seriously, babe? Is this really fucking necessary?" I loved my wife with all my heart. She brought me back to life and had given me two beautiful children whose laughter reminded me of what I once fought for. What I now lived for. But this costume. "This is bullshit. I love you but it is."

Jana laughed from where she was perched on the bed looking sexy as hell dressed up as Velma from Scooby-Doo. "Oh Max, it is so *not* bullshit. You look so good that I'm thinking about saying screw the deposit and keeping this costume. I always had a thing for Superman."

"I hadn't noticed," I grumbled since she always drooled over the damn English dude in the cape. "Halloween is for the kids, not the grownups."

She stood and smoothed down the plaid skirt that gave me pause. Maybe I'd been too hard on Velma as a kid. Those sexy little glasses and that tight fitting sweater definitely made an impression on me. One I couldn't hide in these fucking tights. "Yeah but Halloween night is for grownups and like I said," she leaned in close and pressed her plump tits against my chest as her hands slid up and down my torso with a hungry look in her eyes, "Superman is my favorite."

I groaned out loud when she nibbled my bottom lip, my hands went straight to her ass and pulled her close. "You don't play fair, sweetheart."

"When it comes to having my wicked ways with you? Nevah!" She kissed me again, slow and hard until I was hard and aching everywhere. She pulled back with a sleepy heavy-lidded grin. "Besides, I think this will be more fun than our naked art sessions."

I couldn't stop the groan at the memory of coming home to find big sheets of white paper laid out on the floor with body paint lined up beside it. "I'll be your canvas anytime, Jana."

She kissed me again, harder this time and with more tongue. So much more tongue I groaned and slid my hands under her skirt, slipping a finger inside sexy little panties until I touched her wet pussy and she moaned into me. She clenched around me and I lifted her into the air, ready to send a quick orgasm shooting through her. "Jana," I moaned.

"Yes, Max. Now."

A quiet knock sounded and then a familiar voice. "Mommy, Uncle Lasso stole my cape!" Charlie was on the verge of tears and we both groaned.

"I was so close," she whispered and shimmied down my body with a bit more friction than was necessary.

"I know. I felt how close you were," I told her and slipped my slick middle finger between my lips, making her gasp. "Later we'll talk more about this Halloween for adults."

She laughed and stepped back, smoothing down her hair and then her outfit and readjusting her glasses. "You, husband, have a one track mind."

"And you, wife, turn me into a dirty old man."

Jana's smile softened and she did that sexy little head tilt thing that women did when they were impressed. Or turned on. "I like you dirty." Without another word, Jana left and I stood in the middle of our makeshift room, because we were still on fucking lockdown, wearing a goddamn superhero costume with a fucking hardon.

Great.

Good thing I didn't have to wear it for too long and the truth was, I didn't give a damn what the guys said or thought about it. They'd give me a hard time but Charlie and Jameson would go nuts over it and that was all that mattered. Besides, I didn't think my wife was the only one to have this bright idea. It felt a lot like a conspiracy from the women.

I stepped into the main clubhouse room, all decked out with carved pumpkins that held LED lights because we couldn't have candles around all the kids, paper skeletons, ghosts and witches, it looked like Halloween had thrown up all over the place. The bar, the pool tables and even the Mayhem skull that hung above the bar had been done up to celebrate the holiday. "Holy shit."

"Right?" Teddy stopped beside me and rested her forearm on my shoulder. "We made this place look like a Halloween heaven for the kiddies. You'd never be able to tell this was a place where badass bikers did very serious biker business."

I cocked a brow at her, barely holding in my laugh. "You get weirder every year," I told her seriously.

"Thanks, Max." She pressed up on her toes and kissed my cheek with a laugh. "Jana is gonna eat you alive in that damn thing."

I watched Teddy walk away before heading to the bar to join...the rest of the superheroes. "Glad to see I'm not the only sucker around." Each and every one of the guys was dressed up like a superhero and I couldn't help but laugh.

Golden Boy shrugged, as relaxed as I'd seen him in a long time. Being a family man had done wonders for him, but I knew Teddy was most responsible.

"Haven't you seen how Teddy gets whenever Thor comes on Netflix?"

Savior laughed and clapped Golden Boy's back. "Shit doesn't *come* on Netflix asshole. You have to put it on."

My brother shrugged and took a long pull of his beer. "What do I know? I'm not the computer expert, that's the Black Panther over there." He nodded in Jag's direction, who was dressed up like a more lethal version of the character with a sexy and equally crazy looking Harley Quinn at his side.

"Nice costume," I told Jag with a wide grin.

"Thanks. Harley loves it." He grinned and turned to Vivi, smacking a loud kiss on her lips.

Savior groaned, tugging on the collar of his Captain America uniform. "Why the fuck did I have to dress up? I don't even have any kids."

"Because the kids love the Captain," Cross told him, looking pleased with himself in his Batman uniform. "Smile and look like you're superheroes and not villains."

The men all dispersed but I stayed at the bar and grabbed a shot and a beer. The place looked like a little kid's Halloween party and even though it went against everything the Reckless Bastards was, I couldn't find it in me to give a goddamn. Charlie was giggling up a storm as he stood next to Cross looking like his own little miniaturized version of his favorite superhero. And Jameson was dressed, of course, just like a bottle of Jana's favorite Irish Whiskey. He was giggling so hard he shook in Jana's arms while Rocky pretended to drink him.

How the hell things could be so normal when two of our brothers were missing? I had no fucking clue but I was eternally grateful to the women for keeping life as normal as possible for all the little ones we now had.

"Penny for your thoughts," Vivi said, hip cocked against a stool as she stole my beer.

"Just thinkin' about how good it is to see everyone laughing and smiling in the midst of all this bullshit."

"No kidding. Kids bounce back easily when they're young." She said the words with the weight of someone who knew them personally. "Nice costume, by the way."

"Yeah, thanks. The things we do for love."

"And sex," she added with a snort.

My phone buzzed inside the little pocket at my hip and I struggled to get the damn thing out. "Motherfucker!"

Vivi laugh beside me. "Need some help?"

"No, I got it!" I knew I was being an asshole but the damn thing was so fucking tight. I looked at the screen and groaned. "All that and it's a wrong fucking number."

I was about to reject the call up when Vivi snatched the phone from my hand. "Two missing dudes and a cartel nut remember?" She was right and I nodded.

"Hello?" Her brows furrowed as she listened and then her feet were moving, her fingers snapping in my direction for me to follow her. "It's Vivi and I'm going to help so don't be such a grumpy old asshole or I swear to God, I'll fuckin' leave you stranded."

My shoulders relaxed, and a small smile touched my lips because there was only one person who could make someone that frustrated in under ten seconds.

Gunnar.

Vivi rolled her eyes and turned to me once we were both outside. "I'm going to the camper to help Mr. Grumpy Pants but if you want to gather your bros, they might want to know."

"Bros?"

She rolled her eyes. "That's what you are, right? Now go because I need to get this done before I accidentally put him on a watch list."

She laughed at whatever Gunnar said in her ear and I took a step back and then another until I was damn near running back inside the clubhouse.

"Everything okay?" Jana mouthed when our eyes locked, but I only nodded, eager to get to Cross and the other Reckless Bastards.

"Whoa man, where's the fire?" Savior stepped in front of me, Cross and Jag beside him instantly.

"It's Gunnar. He's on the phone with Vivi. In the camper."

About a thousand questions were shouted at me all at once and I didn't understand any of them. "What about Stitch?"

I shrugged. "I don't fucking know! Vivi took the call and she just said to gather the *bros*."

Jag snickered behind his hands and everyone else frowned at me like I'd lost my damn mind.

Cross smacked his hands together. "Jag and I will go to the camper and get the necessary intel. The rest of you, hang back and watch the families." With those orders, they both strode off, leaving the rest of us to keep the party going.

HOLIDAY HAVOC

Our brothers were alive, and that was reason enough to celebrate for me.

Chapter Eighteen - Cross

"You did a good thing, Cross. The kids had a blast and none of them even realized anything was wrong. Not even Maisie." Moon's strong slender fingers dug into my shoulders, slowly but surely removing every fucking knot in my neck and shoulders. "Relax."

I let out a half-laugh and half-grunt. Moon's ability to see the good side of any shitty situation was just one of the reasons I loved her. Her magic hands were another. "Babe I don't think even three straight days locked in a bedroom with you could get me to relax."

Her melodic laughter sounded in my ears just as her tits pressed up against my back. "Well I'd accept that challenge, but you don't have three days to give me."

There was a smile in her voice but I could also hear the underlying tension and worry there. "I hope to give you all the days when this mess is over." Dealing with the cartel was a bigger mess than my club had ever found ourselves in and I had no fucking clue how we'd get to the other side.

Moon sighed as she dug her knuckles deep into my right shoulder and I could hear the smile in her voice when she spoke. "All the days sound nice but until then, I'd settle for an hour. Or two." She punctuated her words with a gentle, whisper soft kiss behind my ear. On my jawline. "Only if we can get these knots straightened out." Too soon her lips were too far away and her strong hands were back to work, getting me straight for the fight ahead.

"What did I ever do to deserve you, Moon?" I didn't think after Lauren that I deserved this kind of love again but Moon's persistence, her straight talk and her ability to light my body on fire with a single glance, had proven me wrong.

"Maybe you're just lucky." She kissed my cheek again before turning her focus back to the hard knots in my muscles. "Or maybe, Cross, have you ever considered that I'm the lucky one?"

Hell no, I hadn't. Moon was the bright shining star in my life and Beau was the second chance I never thought I'd get. And I wouldn't get to fully explore it if we didn't figure out this shit with the Salinas Cartel. "That's crazy and you know it."

She laughed and we both fell silent. I was lost in thought, thinking about the call from Gunnar that came in almost two days ago. The relief that I felt at hearing from Gunnar, even though he hadn't stayed on the line long enough for me to talk to him, was so immense my knees nearly buckled. They were alive. Barely, according to Vivi who'd relayed their conversation word for word at my request. "Okay, Cross, am I going to have to peel these clothes off in order to get you to relax a little?"

I turned to look at her over my shoulder and smiled at the midnight blue dress she wore that showed off an impressive amount of cleavage even though her soft sweater covered up her incredible arms. Arms I enjoyed watching as they wrapped around me when we kissed, when we made love. Arms that created art as easily as they created meals for her boys or helped take away my stress. "You're amazing, you know that?"

Her face lit up but the love shining in her light green eyes nearly brought me to my knees. "You're pretty amazing too for a guy who's trying to change the subject." Tugging out of the arms of her sweater until her shoulders were bare, she tossed it on the dresser behind her. "Beau is playing with the kids and the door is locked," she told me with a bright smile as one strap of her dress dropped off her slender shoulder. The other fell and seconds later the dress was on the floor, leaving Moon in nothing but a pair of blue lacy panties that did wonderful things for her ass. "Now remember, Cross. This is strictly therapeutic, not at all for your pleasure."

I rose up from the stool I'd been sitting on and went to the bed, dropping down to kick off my boots and then my pants. The rest of my clothes vanished in an instant, firing up the green in her eyes until they were so light they damn near looked clear. "I'll try my best not to enjoy it."

She smiled and pushed at my chest until I was flat on my back, watching her long legs as she climbed on the bed. Straddled me. "Good because therapy is very, very important." Her lips twitched and I swore, I fell even harder for her in that moment. Her ability to make me smile even when shit was as bad as it could possibly be was nothing short of miraculous, and I didn't even believe in miracles.

"Very, ah!" She gripped my cock in her delicate yet capable hands as she slid her slick pussy down over me, enveloping me into her body the same way she'd folded me into her heart. I was lost at the feel of her. The taste of her. The way our scents mingled and swirled in the air to create an unforgettable aroma that fired me up and healed me.

"Cross!" She moaned my name, sobbed it out, roared it and whimpered with my name the only thing on her lips as she rode me. Hard and fast. Insatiable as she pushed us both closer and closer to the top.

I couldn't take my eyes off her, not when just watching her take her pleasure from my body while giving it all back a hundred times over had all the tension seeping from my body. Gripping her hips as she increased the pressure, the intensity of her strokes, I was powerless to turn away from her. The woman who'd given me a thousand different reasons to keep going, to be a better man and a better leader. This woman.

My woman.

"Cross." When she moaned my name the final time, all the tension was gone, replaced by something darker, something hungrier. I flipped our positions so I was on top, wrapping her long legs around me. I thrust into her with so much force we moved the bed. Long, punishing strokes that she took greedily and asked for more. "Please," she begged when I took a beautiful cherry pink nipple in my mouth and sucked hard while I fucked her even harder. "Yes. More! Now!"

I smiled around the plump tit in my mouth, pounding deeper in a frenzy even I couldn't explain, and when she pulsed around me and froze, I knew true fucking bliss in that moment. She squeezed me. Milked me in a tantalizing rhythm that stole my breath. "Moon." The grunt was torn from me the moment her hot wet juices slid between us, increasing the friction and yanking my orgasm right from me. "Ah fuck, Moon!" My entire body went still, then jerked as I spilled deep inside of her while she continued to pulse around me for several long minutes. "You're fucking gorgeous when you come."

Her delighted smile unraveled the last of my tension and when she pulled me down for a long, hot kiss, she drained me completely. "And you look so hot when you come that it makes me want to fuck you all over again."

"I love you, Moon."

Green eyes sparkled with affection. "Cross, I love you too. And I believe you're going to get through this. I really do."

She couldn't have said anything more perfect. "Marry me, Moon." She froze, a shocked look on her face and I cringed. "I take it back," I said hastily.

She frowned, her brows crinkling with confusion. "You don't want to marry me?"

"Don't be stupid, of course I want to marry you. But you deserve a better proposal than that." She deserved something far more romantic than I could ever come up with, but thanks to the rash of marriage and babies within the MC, I had plenty of sources to turn to.

Moon's legs tightened around me and her pussy convulsed around me some more as one foot slid up and down the back of my leg making me shiver. "I don't know, Cross. I can't think of a more memorable way to do it."

"Seriously?"

She nodded slowly but her face was certain. Determined. "Absolutely."

"This will be the proposal just for us, then. Moon, my crazy sexy little hippie chick, will you do me the honor of becoming my wife?"

"Cross, my big bad biker, I can't think of anything I want to do more." Her legs tightened just a little more around me until we were eye to eye, and then she devoured me, slayed me with her sweet, sexy kiss. It turned to something deeper, something hungrier and more intense as the kiss continued on. There was love and passion but there was also something more. Something I couldn't yet describe but something that would sustain me until our lives could find some sense of normalcy.

The door rattled under the pressure of someone's heavy-fisted knock. "Yo, Cross!" Savior's voice was loud and urgent. "We need to talk."

Moon groaned and let her legs fall to my sides. "The President has been summoned." She pulled me down for one more scorching hot kiss before shoving me away. "Go on, big man, lead."

"I fucking love the hell out of you, Moon."

She sighed, wearing a big smile as she laid there in bed, naked and satisfied, looking more beautiful than she ever had. "I love the hell out you too, Cross."

With those words ringing in my head, I got dressed, the smell of Moon still glued to my skin, and got down to fucking business.

The business of kicking ass, taking names, and getting my men back where they belonged.

Chapter Nineteen - Gunnar

Five goddamn days, that was how long Carlito had given us to get this truck filled with his *product* to Reno. What the fuck that product was, we still didn't know for sure. "It's gotta be drugs," Stitch said for at least the ten thousandth time since we'd made it to El Paso, which was ten thousand times too fucking many. I never really understood that statement, familiarity breeds contempt, until I had to walk twenty miles to cross the border.

I was grateful that we'd finally met up with that fat fuck, Guapo. But too much time with Stitch was driving me fucking nuts. And we had another day or two of driving. "No point guessing right now, hopefully we'll get the answers we need soon." Speculating would just be a waste of time when we were headed straight for Mayhem. Hopefully Jag and Vivi would be able to work their geeky magic while the rest of us formed a plan to stop Carlito.

"Yeah, I know but what the hell else are we gonna do?" He was amped up, twitchy with adrenaline and though he wouldn't admit it, Stitch was too worried to sleep. "The view is for shit and there's only country music stations around here," he grumbled again. "Who knew New Mexico and Arizona had so many fucking country music stations?"

That made me laugh because he wasn't wrong and because he was so goddamn irritated by it. "These songs should be right up your alley since they're all about losing your chick and your car, sleeping with somebody else's woman and even getting' your ass beat. Ouch," I groaned when that fucker punched me in my arm. "Your jackoff hand is strong as fuck, man."

Stitch frowned but mischief lit his eyes as he held up his hands. "I only beat off in the shower and lately it's to images of Marisol's sweet little body. Now you, who knows when you last even had a taste of pussy so keep that jackoff arm away from me." He laughed so loud the sound echoed in the truck and even my own lips started to twitch.

"Very fucking funny." We shared another laugh as we drove through the desert. And more fucking desert. Sometime early this morning we'd finally put New Mexico in our rear view and spent most of the day pushing the air-condition less truck through Arizona.

But Stitch was feeling antsy again like a goddamn kid on a long ass road trip. I knew he had something to say but I decided to wait him out because I didn't want to fucking talk anymore, I just wanted to get home and see my kid sister. "You can't blame Marisol for this, Gunnar. It wasn't her fucking fault."

"Never said it was." Yeah, I'd been an asshole about this thing from the beginning but goddamn, the kid could've gotten us killed.

"You didn't," he conceded but his angry undertone was unmistakable. "Not in those exact words but I know you blame her. She came all the way down to Mayhem to warn me that Carlito knew about us and that's when she told me who he was." Stitch raked a hand through his long hair, which he'd finally combed thanks to the money Vivi wired us as soon as we crossed the border into the U.S. and we stopped at a drugstore to buy some shit to get cleaned up.

"Like I said, I don't blame her. I blame you."

"Fuck you, Gunnar!" His fist came down hard on the dashboard. "I can fuck whoever I choose. I don't see you giving shit to Lasso or Savior, who literally brought trouble to our fucking doorstep. You haven't even been around and now all you do is bitch and complain."

He wasn't wrong. Losing my mom hadn't been some big loss for me. She'd barely been a parent to me at all. Hell I was more of a parent to her, picking her up after her latest bender, washing her off and getting her to bed. At least until I figured fighting in wars started by rich men was a way out. But finding out about Maisie had changed my perspective on a lot of shit, especially club shit. I loved my brothers but the constant shit storm was taking its toll. "Yeah well, tough fucking shit, kid."

"I suppose you've never fucked a chick only to find out later that she had a kid or a husband or a warrant for her arrest? Excuse me, you perfect asshole."

"I have a fucking kid to think about, Stitch!" Maisie was all that mattered to me and keeping her safe was my top priority even above the Reckless Bastards MC.

"So fucking what? Lasso has a kid, Max has two and Golden Boy has a kid. Fuck, even Cross has a soon-to-be stepson and none of them are full-time pricks like you." He shook his head and turned to the window. "Fine, Gunnar, it's all my fucking fault. Whatever. How about *you* stay in Mayhem and I'll take care of the rest. Asshole."

"That's not happenin'," I told him honestly but Stitch had finally reached his limit. We drove across Arizona and into Nevada in complete silence and that was just fine by me. I hated talking and I hated emotions and right now, because his girl was in danger, Stitch was a big fucking ball of emotions.

The sun had already set by the time we pulled into the MC compound and I was dog fucking tired. My ass was sore and my legs were numb and I was in desperate need of a real meal. And a fucking shower.

The guys—Cross, Max, Savior, Jag, Black, Golden Boy, Lasso and Lex—all came out to greet us. The women were there too, including Vivi who held my smiling kid sister in her arms, Maisie waving one chubby arm my way. That was all I needed and wanted in this moment. "Baby girl," I said as I approached her.

"Hey big boy, but you should probably call me Vivi since Jag gets all jealous and shit." Vivi giggled and nuzzled my sister—nuzzled her—making her laugh. Who knew Vivi had such a soft spot?

"Very funny," I grumbled at her, but unlike the other women, she only grinned at my pissy mood as she handed Maisie over.

"I thought so and Maisie did too, didn'tcha girl?"

"Vivi!" Maisie blabbered out.

"Gunny's back now so give him a big ol' hug." This woman had such a smart mouth and an air of mischief about her that I knew Jag would have his hands full with her. But she'd also taken a big hit for the club, so I ignored the new nickname.

"Gunny!" Maisie's excited use of the new nickname earned Vivi a glare but she only laughed.

"Thanks," I muttered.

"Don't mention it. She's a sweetheart, unlike her brother. Glad you didn't get killed out there."

"Me too," I told her honestly and held my sister tight. She was almost three years old, talking more each day. Understanding more.

"Gunny stinky." Nothing like the truth from a child to let you know where you really stand.

"Yeah, thanks baby girl." Vivi took her back so I could rinse weeks worth of dirt, blood and grime off me because those fucking motel showers barely had a trickle of water in them. The shower was short and hot but it felt damn good and I had to pull myself out of it because we were on a clock and that motherfucker was tickin'.

I was getting too damn old for this shit and more importantly, Maisie deserved more than a life of uncertainty. A life of constant danger. She deserved to have at least one solid and reliable adult in her life and that had to be me. I had no fucking clue if I could be that or how it would look as long as I was part of the MC, but as soon as this cartel bullshit was over, I would have a good long think about it.

"All right, what do we got?" The guys, and Vivi, had all gathered in the game room of the clubhouse but Jag was suspiciously absent. "Where's Jag?"

"Checking out that truck you came in with. He disabled the GPS," Cross said, sounding tired as hell. "He's checking for any other electronic devices. Stitch already filled us in on everything. Glad you're okay, man."

Okay was the last goddamn thing I was but that wasn't the focus right now. "Better now."

Cross gave a sharp nod and returned to club business. "Vivi and Jag found out quite a bit about Salinas, but anything you can add will help."

"Not much to say. Carlito is a small but crazy motherfucker and he's a punk ass bitch. Scares easily when his men aren't around but his main muscle, Guapo seems loyal as fuck. And violent." That's all I had to add and it seemed like Stitch had already provided that info.

"Did you get any hint they were related, Carlito and Guapo?" Vivi's question seemed deliberate and I wondered what in the hell she was getting at.

"Kind of, I guess. Carlito gave him preferential treatment but that's not saying much since the asshole treats everyone like servants." He must pay his men good money to put up with his shit and the dangers of cartel life.

"They're cousins," Stitch piped in. "I heard them both refer to each other as *primo*," he said, his voice quieter than normal.

"Whoa, look at the kid getting all bi-lingual and shit," Savior joked and clapped him on the back. Stitch smiled back but it was subdued and it came nowhere near reaching his eyes.

"Any hints about his real name?" Vivi was all business as she looked at Stitch, who only shook his head in the negative. "Okay."

Jag yanked the door open and walked in, handing some black contraption to Vivi who typed out a quick code and turned away from us. He flashed her a smile and a wink before turning to Cross. "Good news is there's not enough of a heat signature for people to be inside, thank fuck."

Cross rubbed a hand over his face. "And the bad news?"

"There's an electronic lock on it that has a nine digit code." He cast a look at Vivi who hadn't looked up from that little black box for the past ten or fifteen minutes. "Vivi is trying to see if she can crack it but first we need to figure out how many attempts we get before it shuts us out."

"Or explodes," Vivi added without any trace of humor.

HOLIDAY HAVOC

"Is that a possibility?" Cross was suddenly on alert, his eyes wide and worried since all the women and children were on the compound.

"I mean this *is* a cartel, so yeah, it's always a possibility. Not likely but if you give me a few minutes, I might have some actual answers."

Cross bit his tongue and the rest of us tried to keep our laughter inside, while Lasso outright laughed. "Damn girl you have such a smart mouth!"

"Thanks, Cowboy." Her phone rang and she turned around, whispering quietly as she reached for her laptop. Instead of returning to business, we all sat there and waited. Jag stood by with a smirk on his face while the rest of us watched and waited, hoping good news was on the way. "Okay," she said finally and turned to us. "I need about an hour and I might have some answers on that lock. In the meantime, I got confirmation on that birth certificate." I had an odd feeling of Déjà vu as Vivi told us all about the news reports that had been suppressed and what it meant for Guapo and Carlito.

"Good job, babe." Jag pulled her close and kissed her, long and hard and damn near pornographic in front of the whole MC.

"Anything for you." Her tone was so soft and sweet, her expression so lovestruck it transformed her face and for the first time I could see what Jag saw in her. "Once we hear from Peaches, I'll have a better idea how to get inside that truck."

Cross nodded and stood again. "And we have to get inside that fuckin' truck. We can't risk getting pulled over by the cops or delivering some shit that'll cause blowback on the MC."

"We have about eighteen hours before we have to have this truck in Reno or who knows what the fuck he'll do to Marisol," Stitch added, ignoring the glare I sent his way. In fact, he hadn't looked at me once since we got to Mayhem.

"Don't worry," Vivi said. "Peaches said an hour or less and that's what it'll be."

"Good, thanks Vivi." Stitch stood and turned to Savior. "I need some hardware because Carlito can't be trusted one fucking bit."

Savior nodded and stood, clapping the newbie on his back because he just brought up his favorite topic other than Mandy, guns. "Sure thing. You need anything, Gunnar?"

"Nope. He's staying here," Stitch said, again without looking at me.

"What the fuck, man?" His attitude was starting to piss me off as if we weren't in the middle of a goddamn war with a fucking cartel.

Stitch finally looked at me and the glare was so deadly I thought we might have to fight to clear the air. "You don't want to be involved and now you don't have to. Like you said, this is my fault which means it's *my* fucking problem." Stitch stormed out just as Vivi's phone rang and I fought the urge to roar at the chaos around me.

"Problem, Gunnar?" Cross stared at me, arms folded over his chest and a dark look on his face.

"Nah, the kid's just being sensitive. I said some shit to him and I guess it got to him." It wasn't anywhere near the truth and Cross' expression told me he knew it. "We'll be fine." I hoped.

Vivi ended her phone call and talked in quiet tones to Jag before they both took off, likely for the truck.

Four hours later, Stitch and I were back on the road and headed towards Reno.

In total fucking silence.

Chapter Twenty - Savior

"I can never get enough of you." The words came out of me on a growl as I looked up at my woman, her sex juices smeared all over my face. Mandy's pale skin was all flushed and beautiful from the orgasm that I'd just given her. White blonde hair stuck up in all directions since she'd recently let her pixie cut grow out, giving her the appearance of a sexy little nymph. One that I wanted another taste of.

No, that wasn't right. I *needed* another taste of her. So I took it, leaning forward and sliding my tongue between swollen pussy lips before wrapping my lips around her fat, slick clit. "Mmm, babe. Savior, yes!" Those moans, they always got to me and my cock was already hard, ready to slam into her and make her come again because nothing was as magnificent as Mandy coming apart.

All over my face.

"Oh, God!"

Yeah, that was the sound I couldn't get enough of, so I just closed my eyes and let my lips and my tongue do the work. She was so damn primed from her last orgasm that she shot off like a rocket, fast and out of this fucking world. "Mandy."

"Savior," she grinned as I climbed up her body, dotting her sensitive skin with kisses until I got her mouth. "You're teasing me."

"I am but only because it's one of my favorite things to do." I never thought about shit like falling in love, not even when I was falling in love with the woman in my arms, pressing her soft lips to the crook of my neck, but Mandy turned me into someone else.

She pushed at my chest, her smile full of mischief. "Then it's only fair that I return the favor, right?" Before I could say another word her lips moved down my body but it was the weight of her tits, the pressure of her hard tipped nipples as they scraped down my body that totally fucking unraveled me. "Mmm." That hum of pleasure as she fisted my cock, like she was enjoying this as much as me, made me grow even harder.

Fuck, I was so goddamn hard it took everything in me not to thrust into her mouth and fuck it. The way Mandy gave head, like it was as erotic for her as it was for me, always sent me to another fucking planet. Another world that only reminded me that women like her existed and a few lucky bastards out there—like me—got to experience a passion like this. "Oh fuck!"

She released me with a smack of her lips and smiled. "That must be the spot," she laughed and before I could respond she had her lips wrapped around me again, taking me deep. My hips began to move on their own but instead of backing off, she took more of me until the tip of my cock hit the back of her throat. "Mmm," she moaned around me and I was lost.

Gone.

Adrift in a sea of sensations too powerful to put a name too. Hell, too powerful to do anything but experience them. Experience the feel of her warm, wet lips wrapped around my cock, the scrape of her tongue that sent ripples of electricity through my veins.

"Fuck. Sweet fucking Mandy." She moaned like the sound of my voice turned her on, like my cock was the only thing she needed to be happy. "Oh fuck, baby. Yeah." She took me deep and swallowed, squeezing a vise around my cock until my spine began to tingle. The tip of her tongue slid along the underside of my nut sac and I was a fucking goner.

My body trembled and convulsed as pleasure erupted out of me. Every pore was on fire while Mandy drank me dry, and then she kept sucking just because the little fucking tease loved to hear me moan. "That almost makes us even."

I laughed and pulled her up so we were face to face, side by side, labored breaths mingling together and wearing matching smiles. "If we're even that means I owe you another," I told her, making her laugh.

"Too bad you don't have the time for that." Her smile dimmed just a little as worry clouded big green eyes because she knew this time together, amazing as it was, had neared its end. "Be careful."

"I'm always careful, babe." Both of my hands reached around her and grabbed her ass so every inch of her silky skin was flush against me. "Let's not talk about that now, tell me about your good news."

She smiled. "You distracted me masterfully, babe." Her lips brushed my jaw softly and I shivered. "My chocolate line has done so well that Drake wants me to create a signature box of chocolates for the casino!" Her face lit with happiness and I couldn't deny that I wore an equally goofy fucking grin.

"Damn baby, that's fucking great!" She'd worked hard to get Drake to let her sell her own creations under her name, and it had done so well that she was now *the* confectioner in all of Las Vegas. "Congratulations. Does this warrant a congratulatory lick?"

Mandy's head fell back and soft wisps of blonde hair hit the black pillows in my bedroom at the clubhouse. "I got plenty of licks and gave a lot too so don't worry. It's really fucking exciting though, right?"

"So exciting, babe. Feel free to drip the chocolate on me if you need a tester." Another great thing about falling in love with a pastry chef? All the fucking sweets that were constantly around. "Maybe more of that body paint you made." That had been a fun fucking night and I could tell she was thinking about it too by the way her skin flushed pink.

"It was just chocolate, Savior, with food brushes. I'll break that out when you come back to me. Safe and in one piece." This woman could slay me like no other.

"You seriously think I'm gonna let some stupid fucking cartel assholes stop me from making it back to you? There is no one on this fucking planet that could keep me from you."

"Good." She sighed and sat up, turning to me when I sat up beside her. Mandy cupped my jaw with one hand, love and worry written all over her beautiful face. "Because it's not just me relying on you anymore, Savior." Her words lingered in the air between us for several long fucking moments, hanging in the air.

Thick and terrifying. I knew I was going to be a father and I was still adjusting to the idea.

"Mandy, babe, say the words. Tell me right out."

"We're having twins. Twins!" She blew out another breath. "I know this isn't the ideal time to tell you but now it looks like this cartel shit might go on for a while and well, I didn't want to add to your stress."

Oh, fuck that. "Baby you never add to my stress. You are the only person that takes it all away. Always." All the tension fled her body at my words and I turned into her hand, kissing the center of her palm. "We're having fucking twins. Two babies. I can't fucking believe it." The idea of one baby had me popping antacids like a man on death row, the idea of two was so fucking terrifying I had no frame of reference for it. Not war. Not biker war. Nothing.

"But you're happy, right?"

"Are you serious?" I cupped her face in my hands, smiling so damn big I thought my mouth might split at the corners. "Over the fucking moon!" That was the truth and though I would like to have put a ring on her finger first, I wouldn't change a damn thing about any of it. "We're having two fucking babies!"

She finally laughed so hard her shoulders shook. "Our kids are going to have such fucking potty mouths."

Our kids. "I love the sound of that, our kids. When are these little rugrats coming?"

"Well I'm ten weeks, so...doc says beginning of July. Are you really happy about this, Savior? I know the pregnancy was unexpected and exciting, but twins—"

I pressed three fingers to her mouth, chuckling a little at the frown she sent my way. "There's nothing to not be happy about. You're mine and I'm yours and I put two babies in you." She rolled her eyes with an affectionate smile. "As soon as life gets back to normal I'm going to put a ring on that fucking finger to make it forever."

She softened at my words like they were exactly what she needed to hear from me. "I love you, Savior. Please be safe and come back to me. To us."

"I promise," I told her and I fucking meant it.

***

The entire ride to Reno, I couldn't help but think about my girl. About our change in circumstances. I wanted to marry her, hell, today if I could. But considering we were all headed up to Reno to possibly go head to head with a fuckin' cartel boss, I couldn't.

I couldn't ask Mandy to marry me when I knew there was a chance I might not make it out of this shit alive. She'd already lost too much. Everything. Her brother and my club brother, Ammo. Her parents. Losing me might break her completely and I couldn't have that shit on my conscious.

So, I had to be the bigger, badder, crazier bastard to make sure that whatever happened now, I made it back to my girl. And our babies.

About thirty minutes outside of Reno, I had to clear my mind. It was essential in our line of work, and survival depended on it. So I pushed Mandy out of my mind and got into warrior mode. We had no clue what, if anything, would go down when Gunnar and Stitch dropped off that fucking truck but with cartels, death was always an option. I wouldn't put anything past this Carlito asshole based on everything Vivi had dug up on him and his whole operation.

The only thing that made me worry was my brothers, Gunnar and Stitch. There was some beef brewing between them and in a situation like this, underlying tension could get us all killed. Cross knew what he was doing and I had every confidence in him, but his brain had to be sex addled for him to let them drive up together. Whatever had gone down between them, I just hoped it didn't bite us all in the ass at the worst possible time.

I pulled into the parking lot where Gunnar and Stitch were supposed to meet Carlito and spotted Lex's ginger hair standing well above the crowd waiting for the bingo hall to open. He gave me a discreet nod and I parked my bike as close as I could to the door and joined him so we could walk in together. "Been here long?"

"Nah, I circled the block a few times to see if anything stuck out for me. It didn't so I mingled with the seniors." He sent a flirty finger wave to a group of older women who erupted in a fit of giggles. "Apparently they know the delights that can be found in the bed of a ginger." He wiggled his eyebrows and I laughed.

We got settled with bingo cards and ink, right by the window so we could watch. Inconspicuously. Twenty minutes later Lasso pulled up and went inside the Oriental Dragon and ten minutes later he was joined by Jag. Most of the MC who'd been tasked with coming up to Reno was in place.

Now all we had to do was wait.

And I fucking hated waiting.

Chapter Twenty-One - Lasso

"How long do you think this asshole is gonna make us wait?" Jag and I sat inside some generic Chinese food buffet, right by the windows with our eyes focused on the cube truck Gunnar and Stitch leaned against. Smoking cigarettes.

He lifted his shoulders casually and let them fall, but I wasn't confused by his attempt to appear unaffected. "Who knows? Probably as long as he feels like it, especially if Stitch stole his girl."

"I gotta see this chick because I'm curious as fuck how scrawny ass Stitch was able to snatch a babe from a cartel boss!" Not that I doubted the kid's prowess since I was pretty sure he'd already gotten busy with our pretty attorney, Tanya.

"She could be fucking homely, Lasso." Jag's lips twitched because he knew that was bullshit. "Or maybe she thinks the kid's her key out of that life." He shook his head and bit into an eggroll. "She wouldn't be far off, the Bastards have an inordinate amount of men with hero complexes."

"It's not a complex when you're a real goddamn hero." He laughed. Both of our gazes kept sliding to the truck at the far end of the parking lot just in case any shit popped off. "So, *Jeremiah*, what are your plans now that Vivi has returned?"

His smile spread, big and wide. "I'm going to marry her as soon as shit around here dies down." That certainty was so typical of Jag. The man never met a challenge he couldn't overcome.

"Don't you think you should ask her first?" Rocky and I had gotten married purely out of necessity the first time around so I knew how important it was to do it right.

"I'll ask, but she'll say yes. Vivi loves me." And the rest of us loved seeing that his smile had returned.

"Good because you were a miserable fucking bastard for the past year. And just because she loves you doesn't mean you don't have to go all out and give her a big, special proposal." He laughed.

"I know how to ask her how to marry me, man."

"Aww, man, I have a great idea. Hack the President's teleprompter and ask her."

Jag barked out a laugh and shook his head. "Nah, she'd never forgive me for that. Probably would kill me her damn self." His gaze turned back to the truck as a black SUV pulled into the lot but turned out to be another group of old ladies headed for the Bingo hall. "I'll find some way to do it right." I had no doubt he would.

I nodded and took a few bites of my own food. "You got any idea what's up with Gunnar and Stitch?" The tension between them was pretty fucking hard to ignore and it was more than just the shit they'd been through together in Mexico.

After he finished a bite of fried rice, Jag shrugged and leaned back in his chair. "My guess is that Gunnar was being his typical asshole self, blaming Stitch for something he couldn't have possibly known. The same way he blamed you for Rocky. Me for Vivi."

I nodded because we'd have to be blind not to see that the Gunnar who'd returned was a bigger asshole than the one who left to look after his dying mother. "Think we should be worried?" No one had said a thing but we were all worried about how the anger between them would affect our moves today.

Jag nodded and wiped his hands on a napkin. "He hasn't been himself since he got back. I can't explain it but it's like he's twitchy or something. Like he wants out of the Bastards. I wonder what he's thinking." Leaving the club was a big fucking deal and not something that was done lightly.

"Yeah, I think he's got something going on. But Stitch? That kid is a true blue Reckless fucking Bastard. Bringing us a damn good weed supply *and* a war with the cartel all in his first fucking year." I took another bite.

"I'm surprised you're so relaxed about it considering you have a family to worry about, now." Jag said, scooping up a bite in his chopsticks.

I shrugged it off. "This is the life of a cowboy, Jag. We're always fighting some fucking outlaw or other bad guy and saving strong-willed damsels in distress. I chose this life with my eyes wide open. We all did."

"Even with a wife and kid?"

"Kids," I clarified, sharing the good news with my best friend.

"No shit? You're having another kid. That's fuckin' great, Lasso." His bright white smile lit up his whole face. "Congrats, man."

"Thanks. We just found out a couple days ago. With all of us turning into old men, getting' hitched and having babies, it's more important than ever for the Bastards to keep winning. We have more to fight for. More to live for."

That didn't mean that I wasn't scared as fuck about fighting with the cartel because those fuckers were ruthless. Pointlessly violent, raping and killing just for the hell of it. Or in retaliation. "When you're in the club, you can't half-ass it, you know that better than most. You have to be willing to do what it takes for your club and your family. Look what Vivi did for you, fuck for all of us. That's family. That's hardcore fucking family, man."

Jag's lips twitched, half in amusement and half in pride. "Fuck Lasso, when did you get so deep?"

"Apparently when I met Rocky. Falling in love makes you strong as fuck and since I was already strong as fuck, I'm damn near invincible. And arrogant," I told him with a smile. "Rocky always says I'm too cocky to die."

"She's right about that," he agreed with a quick smile and stacked his empty plates on the edge of the table. "Don't worry, Cowboy, I've got your back."

"Damn straight!"

Jag's smile faded and he started to rise from his seat. "Look alive, Lasso. We've got three black SUVs turning into the lot." Then he was on his feet, an expression of pure steel on his face. When the first couple emerged from the lead SUV, Jag groaned. "Fuck me. I don't know whether to be relieved or fucking frustrated."

"Better to be a bunch of old couples going dancing at the Community Center than a carload of psychotic Mexican cartel members."

"Yeah but the longer it takes him to show up, the more antsy I get." Jag scrubbed a hand over his head and grunted. "This waiting is driving me fucking crazy."

I knew what he meant but an hour later, this Carlito guy still hadn't shown up.

Or the hour after that.

Even I was starting to think the asshole wouldn't show.

KB WINTERS

Chapter Twenty-Two - Stitch

Ten goddamn hours. That's how long Carlito kept us waiting before he showed his stupid fucking face, showing up with a caravan of black SUVs. He strutted up in his white denim pants and a big ass cowboy hat, belt buckle, a light pink shirt complete with a fucking bolero tie that had a humongous turquoise rock in the center. Pointy toe Italian style boots completed the look. His smile was smug, so fucking pleased with himself for making everyone wait on him, I wanted to pound his face into the fucking cement. "Motherfucker," I grumbled under my breath, ignoring Gunnar's heavy breathing beside me.

The big man was seething and I knew we'd have to be careful until I set eyes on Marisol. He pushed off the side of the truck, squaring his wide shoulders and standing at his full height. "It's about goddamn time. Where the fuck is the girl?"

The girl? I scoffed but kept my thoughts to myself. Gunnar was a stubborn son of a bitch and there was no point getting myself riled up over shit I couldn't change. But I stood next to Gunnar because, right now, we were a team.

Carlito's smarmy grin spread when his fat fucking henchman appeared at his side. He took a step back when Gunnar took a step forward. "She is here. Where is my shipment?"

"Inside the big fucking truck *you* gave us, shit for brains." Gunnar snorted out a bitter laugh and crossed massive arms across his wide chest. The man was a beast and the only signs of intelligence Carlito showed, was being afraid of him. "Show us the girl and you'll get your fucking truck."

His brown eyes studied Gunnar and me for a long time before he turned and whispered something in Spanish to Guapo, who went back to the middle SUV and pulled Marisol out, much harder than he fucking needed to.

She was pale and her thick dark hair was matted to one side of her head and her wrists were tied together with zip ties. My hands gripped into tight fists when she looked up and lifted her hands to shield her eyes against the sun, brushing hair from her face to reveal a big fucking purple bruise on her right eye. Marisol's jeans and t-shirt were filthy and all I could think was that he'd kept her in that same fucking room all this time.

It took everything in me not to bridge the gap between me and that sorry fucker and turn his face into fucking hamburger meat. "You tiny little asshole," I growled at him. I couldn't believe this little shit was the boss of the cartel. He was such a pussy.

"Watch your temper," Carlito warned, eyes trained on me with a small smile tilting his thin lips upward.

I pushed my boots into the blacktop parking lot as hard as I could to keep myself rooted to the ground until this fucking trade was over. "Watch yourself, little man."

Gunnar grunted and stepped between us. "Enough with this fucking bullshit! Give me the girl and take your shit. Now." He looked so goddamn intimidating that even I almost flinched.

Guapo stepped forward to protect his boss. Or his cousin. Or his boyfriend, who the fuck knew at this point. He put a hand up to Gunnar's chest and just that quick, Gunnar twisted his wrist until he was on his knees. "*Puto cabrón*," he spat, eyes full of hatred as he stared up at Gunnar.

"You got something you want to say, fat boy?" When Guapo said nothing, Gunnar grinned. "Tell your ape to keep his fucking hands to himself. Next time I'm keepin' one of 'em." Even I believed that crazy bastard.

Carlito clapped his hands like a fucking spinster aunt. "Calm down, boys. Now you see the girl is here, I want my shipment."

Gunnar cast a quick glance at Marisol, just long enough to take in her unkempt appearance before sending a harder, angrier look at Carlito. "She ain't in the condition we agreed on, Carlito."

"Yes, well, Marisol has a hard time following instruction." The smug bastard was so goddamn creepy, I couldn't wait to get my hands on him, especially when Marisol shivered like she was cold in this seventy-five-degree weather. She looked beaten. Exhausted. Terrified.

"She ain't the only one," Gunnar said, taking another step forward when Guapo finally got back to his feet. "How you gonna fix this, Carlito?"

His thick dark brows furrowed in confusion. "Fix what? She is here."

"But *not* unharmed. I thought you said you were a man of your word."

Carlito laughed but he couldn't hide the fear in his eyes. He might be crazy but only when he had the advantage. "Fix? What do you propose?"

Gunnar grinned and it was a terrifying, snarly grin. Like a lion right before that motherfucker pounced. "Well I would propose you let us put Guapo out on the stroll, but I don't think too many men out there want to fuck a big fat fucking teddy bear." He next words were cut off when Guapo sent a fist flying into Gunnar's gut. "Damn you hit like a bitch, maybe we'll just put you in one of the whore houses so you can give out five-dollar blow jobs."

Guapo lifted his fist again, hate shining so bright his eyes were black but it was a mistake. Another one. Gunnar's fist was raised higher and he let it go with a sickening crack to that fucker's jaw.

"*Puto!*"

Another King Kong sized fist raised in the air and Guapo braced himself for the hit that never came. He opened his eyes to find Gunnar right in his face, nostrils flaring and face red, prepared to throw down. "You want to do this, fat boy? Because I will fucking rip your tiny cock out through your throat."

Carlito hissed at his henchman. "*Guapo, calmate no hay tiempo .*"

HOLIDAY HAVOC

"We waited plenty of fucking time," I told him. "You have time now for your boy to get the beatdown he deserves. You next?"

He froze and gave Guapo a quick head nod, sending the man back to his feet where he grabbed Marisol and shoved her in my direction. Carlito jumped into the passenger seat of the first SUV and rolled down the window. "Next time I tell you to come alone, you do it!" He pointed at Gunnar, who he'd pegged as our leader.

Gunnar stared at Carlito until he squirmed in his seat, sweat beading around his hairline. "There won't be a fucking next time, asshole. If I see either one of you again, I won't hesitate to put a bullet in your fucking head. And yours," he pointed at Guapo who now occupied the driver's seat. "Get the fuck outta here."

I waited, hand on the piece holstered behind me, certain this dirty motherfucker would try to be tough before he left. Instead, Guapo hit the gas and the SUVs surrounded the truck and got to work.

"Let's go," Gunnar said, wrapping a protective arm around Marisol and leading her across the parking lot to the plain black van behind the strip mall.

Thank fuck this shit was over. For now.

I hoped.

HOLIDAY HAVOC

Chapter Twenty-Three - Max

The thing no one ever said about falling love, about having a family, was how their pain became your pain. Since having children and getting married, I had a greater appreciation for what my own ma went through, raising two hellions like me and Golden Boy. Watching Jana in the clubhouse kitchen—where she'd been for the past four hours straight—rinsing and chopping, boiling and sautéing, baking and frying, brought new meaning to the word *pain*.

She hadn't stopped moving since she woke up. Hell, if I was keepin' it real, she hadn't stopped for the past twenty-four hours when she'd taken Marisol in her arms and got her cleaned up and in some new clothes. The sight of the poor woman, frail and broken, had touched something inside of my woman. I just hoped it was temporary. "Babe, relax. Please." I wrapped my arms around her from behind and startled the fuck out of her, proof of just how deep into her thoughts she'd been.

"Max," she sighed, letting her weight relax against me. "Where did you come from?"

"I've been watching you for a while, baby. Talk to me." I turned her in my arms and held her chin so her gorgeous green eyes were on me.

"What do you want me to say? The shit she must have gone through, Max." Tears pooled in her eyes as she dropped her head to my chest and fisted her hands in my shirt. I wrapped my wife in my arms and held her while she cried, our kids playing in the corner because she hadn't let them out of her sight for the past two days. "She has bruises everywhere, some healed with new bruises on top of them, and even a few cuts. Shallow cuts but there was one deep cut," her words broke off, no doubt thinking of the event that caused the deep scar on one side of her face that I barely noticed anymore.

"She's okay now, babe. And if she's not, she will be. Stitch will make sure of it." The kid had stepped up, big fucking time. Gone was the playful new Bastard we all loved, replaced by the serious, take no shit man who looked after his woman.

"There's no being okay after that, Max. Trust me." I wished there was some way I could erase the memory of what she'd gone through with her foster father. Better yet, I wished I could find that motherfucker and give him the ass kicking of a lifetime and leave him with his own personal scars.

"You know I do, baby. But don't shut down on me, please. I need you and our boys need their ma. If you want, help Marisol. I have a feeling she's gonna stick around for a while."

Jana cast a glance at our boys, who'd finally played themselves into exhaustion, curled up together in the playpen. Asleep. "You'd never be able to tell what terrors they are when they're sleeping," she laughed.

"Just wait," I told her, making her shiver with unease.

"If they're half as bad as you and Golden Boy, I'm handing the reigns over to you, honey." There was nothing I loved more when she pressed on my shoulders to lift her petite frame up and took the kiss she wanted.

"Mmm, reigns," I moaned against her mouth, using my body to press hers against the counter and taking our kiss to the next level. It started slow and sweet, but then, her slick pink tongue slipped between my lips and cranked up the heat to about a thousand degrees. When her arms wrapped around my neck, I lifted her up and let myself get lost in the taste of her. Happy to see her fears didn't leave a lasting damage.

Too soon, she pulled back. "Is this cartel shit over now, Max?"

I hoped to fucking hell that the answer was yes, but the truth was I really didn't know. But the truth I couldn't tell my wife was, I didn't think this was over. Not yet, anyway. "Until we have a reason to think it isn't, yeah babe, it's over."

Jana's eyes searched my face for signs of deception because I promised I would never lie to her, not even to ease her mind. "But you don't think it is?"

"It's the cartel babe. They don't usually give up easily but let's not borrow any trouble, yeah?" Brushing a lingering kiss to her forehead, I held Jana close until her arms went around my waist and she relaxed against me. "I won't ever let anything happen to you, baby."

She nodded against my chest. "I know, and I love you for it. But I can't stop thinking about Marisol. God, she must have been so terrified." How could I not love this woman with every fucking fiber of my being? Instead of being angry at Marisol for bringing this trouble and potential danger to our doorstep, to our fucking family, she was worried about her. Afraid for her.

"I'll check with Stitch and see how she's doing, okay? Maybe you can go up there and see her yourself." I knew it was the only thing that would make her feel better and allow her to get back to being the wife and mom our family needed her to be.

"I love you, Max."

"Damn straight you do, babe. I love you more." And that was the fucking truth.

Jana grabbed my shoulders and slid from the counter, those damn fine curves she hadn't been able to lose since giving birth to Jameson pushed up against me and sent blood shooting straight to my cock. "That's good to hear. Now back up so I can finish all of this," she spread her hands around the kitchen, filled with all kinds of dishes from chicken and sausages, to mac & cheese, salad and a few dozen cookies.

"You know Thanksgiving isn't for another week or so, right?" There was enough food to feed the entire club, the Reckless Bitches and the families for at least a few days.

Her sweet laugh echoed in the kitchen, causing Charlie to stir in his sleep. "I needed something to keep from going crazy and unfortunately, spread sheets weren't getting the job done." Between feeding everyone and tending to her clients, I didn't know when she found time to sleep but she was the perfect wife. Able to hold shit down when I couldn't and she never complained, just wrapped her arms around me happily when I returned. "And you were occupied."

I growled against her neck and nibbled her ear. "I'll get Lex to watch the boys and we can take an hour or so for ourselves." After the past few weeks, that was exactly what I needed. An hour alone with my woman.

"Give me an hour and then I'm all yours, big guy." Then Jana jumped up and wrapped her legs around my body, crashing her mouth against mine in a kiss so hot I would have taken her right there in the kitchen if not for the sleeping boys in the corner.

When she pulled back, I smacked her ass with a groan. "I'm gonna hold you to that, sweetheart."

Chapter Twenty-Four - Gunnar

Goddamn it was good to be home. Not even when I left to take care of my mom and get custody of Maisie had I missed Mayhem as much as I did over the past few weeks. Being back now, though, I appreciated every little thing. From getting up at the ass crack of dawn because for some reason that was when tots liked to wake up, to trying to navigate breakfast with a fussy little tyrant whose blue eyes matched my own. "Gunny, more 'cakes!"

If she wasn't the most adorable damn kid on the planet I'd have fed her oatmeal with no butter or brown sugar. Instead, in my efforts to be the parent she deserved, I'd made pancakes. Blueberry pancakes, thank you very much. Brother of the fucking year. "We already had pancakes for breakfast, Maisie."

I watched as she got comfortable on her perch at the top of the slide. She nibbled her bottom lip in concentration as she prepared to launch herself from the top. She was an outside baby, preferring to be out in the sun and playing in the dirt than doing anything indoors.

Finally, she launched herself down the plastic incline, giggling loudly as she picked up speed and flew right into my arms. "More 'cakes Gunny!" She smacked a loud kiss to my cheek before wiggling out of my arms and running around to repeat the steps all over again. And again.

And again.

The energy she had was astounding. Hell, the truth was, I envied that level of energy. Compared to her, I felt like an old man, constantly dragging ass while she darted around full of life and excitement. But this was parenting so I stood my ass at the foot of the slide and caught her at least a dozen more times. "No more pancakes," I told her, using the sternest voice I was capable of with her, which wasn't nearly as stern as it was with the rest of the world.

"Catch me, Gunny!" She pushed herself off the slide with as much power as her chubby little arms would allow and came flying at me, right into my waiting arms.

"Love you, mwah," she said as she pressed a kiss to my cheek to accompany the sound.

"Love you too, squirt." Having kids was never something that I'd thought would be my life. I didn't have a good example and given my life with the Reckless Bastards, I just didn't think it was possible. But meeting Maisie had changed all that. I loved her from the moment she looked up at me with those big blue eyes that we both got from our mother. A protective instinct rose up in me, and when Ma asked me to give her a better life than she'd given me, I knew I would.

"Push, Gunny?" Her little mouth pursed into an adorable half-pout, half-smile as her eyes drifted to the swing set about twenty feet away from the slide.

I put her on the ground and Maisie took off, her chubby little legs encased in denim carried her to the row of five swings. "Wait for me, squirt."

"Push high," she instructed when I stopped in front of her and lifted her in the air to plop her in the swing seat. I was powerless against her smile but when I stood behind and pushed her higher and higher, the sound of her giggles wrapped me around her tiny little fingers. When she looked at me like I was some kind of hero, it only strengthened my resolve that I needed to find a way to keep her safe. To give her better than we ever got.

"Head up, Maisie." She loved to lean back with wild abandon and even two tumbles out of the swing hadn't cured her of it, even if both times had shaved a few years off my life.

"But the sky, Gunny! Sooo pretty!"

I swear, that sweet giggle would be the death of me. The sound of a car door slamming stole my attention and put me on immediate alert.

"Time to go inside."

"But, Gunny—"

"We'll come back later, squirt. I promise." That shut her up quickly and I scooped her from the swing, and with her hanging from my hip, we marched in long-legged strides to the back door entrance of the clubhouse. "Ask Uncle Cross to come outside, okay?"

"Okay. Love you, Gunny!" It was her way of saying goodbye but this time she managed a wave while running on unsteady legs and that little move pulled another smile from me.

When I was sure she wouldn't sneak out for more time on the swings, I turned to the woman who now leaned against a sleek black Tesla SUV that looked like it came from outer fucking space.

She was curvy as fuck with honey brown skin that said she was mixed race or maybe Latina. Confidence oozed from her in painted on blue jeans and a white t-shirt that hugged big round tits and a slender waist, but her wild burgundy curls said she was a force to be reckoned with. My cock twitched to life, surprising the fuck outta me since I hadn't been with a woman since a few random hookups after my mom had passed. It had been so long I almost didn't recognize the sensation.

But just as quickly as my cock sprang to life, so did my unease. Strangers didn't just show up at the compound and definitely not through the back gate when it was locked. Oversized sun glasses shielded her eyes but I could tell they were trained on me by the way her pouty red mouth curved into a smile. And because I felt her gaze as it raked over my body. "Can I help you?" Dammit, I sounded gruff as fuck, as usual, but I didn't know this chick or who'd sent her. No matter how fuckin' hot she was.

"Maybe, but right now I have more important matters to deal with." My darkest scowl didn't even faze her, her own smile just grew wider.

"Look lady, I don't have time for your fucking games. Why are you here and how the hell did you get in?"

One brow cocked high above her sunglasses and then she removed them, revealing amber eyes that were so light she looked otherworldly, or some shit.

"I'm here—" she began but her words cut off at the sound of the door smacking open behind me.

"Holy shit, Peaches, you're here! And you look damn good, girl."

Vivi. I should have fucking known. This woman, no matter how talented, was the walking, talking definition of trouble. Chaos. The woman, Peaches, smiled even brighter. "Same girl, love agrees with you. And I'm diggin' the pink hair!"

Before her words were even out of her mouth, Vivi brushed past me at a run, stopping in front of the curvy beauty and wrapping her skinny arms around her in a tight hug. "You said you might be able to fly in a few days from now or else I would've picked you up from the airport."

Peaches threw her head back and laughed, showing off a freckle right over the pulse of her neck. "My new ride came in the day we spoke and I figured this was the perfect trip to test it out. What do you think?" She stepped back and I watched them both in wide-eyed fascination as Vivi circled the car, brushing a finger along it reverently.

I'd never seen women get so enthralled by a car. It was kind of a fucking turn-on. "Damn this thing is sweet as fuck, Peaches. Business must be good."

"Damn good," she replied with a shrug. "Anyway I didn't think it was a good idea to catch a commercial flight with all the sketchy shit I got with me so, here I am." Peaches ran a hand through her hair, fluffing her curls as she took in her surroundings with the keen eyes of someone who was used to trouble. It made me curious about her story.

"Sketchy shit, I'm intrigued." Vivi smiled and looked at her friend and it was the softest I'd ever seen her. I could see why Jag had fallen for her.

"You will be," Peaches promised and squinted her eyes in my direction, licking her lips. "Hey, Big Sexy, think you can use those muscles to help me with something?"

Fuck yeah, but…Big Sexy? "I'm not a valet."

"Good," she said and rolled her eyes, "because I'm not offering a tip." She waited a beat but instead of pouting or begging, she turned and lifted the badass bat wing side door of the SUV and bent over, giving me a long and satisfying glimpse of her heart-shaped ass. She heaved out a suitcase with a loud grunt. With a casual kick, she tilted the box on its wheels and smiled at Vivi. "Anywhere we can have some privacy?"

"Yeah. Our camper is over here because lockdown is still in full effect. You can meet Jag later, for now just follow me."

Peaches fell in step beside her after she closed the batwing door, and they talked and laughed loudly as they crossed the parking lot toward the camper. She stopped when Maisie shot out the door and stepped in front of them. "Hey cutie, who do you belong to?"

Maisie grinned and pointed my way. "Gunny!"

Peaches looked over her shoulder at me, giving me another long up and down look that she punctuated with a wink. "Lucky girl."

"I like your hair," the little girl said as she pointed to the wild curls.

"I like yours too," she offered, twirling a finger around one of her curly pigtails.

Vivi knelt down in front of Maisie, who hugged her with all her might. "This is my friend Peaches. Peaches meet Maisie, Gunny's kid sister."

Peaches held her hand out until Maisie took it. "Nice to meetcha, Maisie."

My little sister giggled when Peaches shook her hand like she was an adult. "Nice to meetcha too, Peaches. That's a funny name."

"It's because I'm so sweet," she shot back with a smile that made the little girl laugh even harder.

"You're funny. Wanna play?"

She looked at me and then back to Maisie. "Maybe later, kiddo. I've been driving for a long time and I need a nap."

"Grown-ups don't have to take naps," she accused.

"No, but why wouldn't you want to curl up in bed in the middle of the day?" With that thought she gave her pigtail a gentle tug and kicked her box back on its wheels. "Don't forget about our playdate later, okay"

Vivi whispered in Maisie's ear and sent her running to me while she herded Peaches into her camper just as Jag came out and laid a hand on my shoulder. "I see you met Peaches."

"Yeah," I grunted.

"She's funny," Maisie said to Jag, arms raised in the universal sign for pick me up.

Jag picked her up and blew a raspberry on her cheek. "Jana's finally done cooking, who's hungry?"

"Me!" Maisie clapped her hands excitedly and gestured for me to join her and Jag.

Food. That was music to my fucking ears.

Chapter Twenty-Five - Stitch

"We got breakfast burritos, spicy home fries with Jana's delicious salsa and a few pastries that Mandy whipped up before work." I said as I brought in a tray of food.

How in the hell Jana found the energy to cook all this food every day for the past few days, I'd never know. But I was grateful that she had because the kitchenette in the club's apartment Cross had been living in until about six months ago when he moved in with Moon, was bare. That and I was shit in the kitchen beyond grilled cheese and SpaghettiOs.

Marisol's brown eyes widened in surprise but that haunted look still lingered there. "I hope no one went through all this trouble on my behalf." Her voice was soft and quiet, almost timid in a way I'd never heard from her.

"What, like you're not worth it?" I shook my head, ignoring the sad look in her eyes that was like a kick to the fucking nuts. "Jana has been stressed and to deal, she's been cooking up a storm for the past couple days. This is what she does when she's stressed."

Her lips twitched in a smile, but the old Marisol still hadn't emerged. Not after spending a few hours with Jana, who got her cleaned and changed after spending over a week with that fucking tiny psychopath. "That's kind of her. And you. Thanks, Stitch."

"None necessary, babe. Just dig into this feast before I eat it all and ruin my figure." That pulled another small smile from her but it was a small flicker compared to the woman I'd met six months ago. I appreciated that Cross had given us his old place during the lockdown because Marisol was too traumatized, too broken right now to mix in with the chaos of the MC. We'd been up here for going on four days, the first two of which were spent mostly in total silence because Marisol refused to speak.

Even now, when she did speak it was so damn soft I could barely hear her. Or worse, it was shaky as though she was on the verge of tears. She still refused to talk to me about what had happened during that week when we were apart but I'd somehow found a reserve of patience for her. I wouldn't push hard but I would still push.

She got up quietly and I groaned at the sight of her, fully dressed. Marisol had gone out of her way to hide her body from me over the past few days which only heightened my suspicions about what that fucktard had done to her. She must've gotten dressed while I was out getting food from downstairs, dammit.

"Thank you," she whispered again when got settled at the small kitchen table. At first she ate hesitantly, like she was waiting for something bad to happen, which only made me more curious to know what that bastard had done to her.

I was happy to see her appetite return as she tucked into half of a big ass steak and egg burrito, pouring a healthy serving of Jana's habanero salsa over the top of it. "Damn girl, I love to watch you eat."

"Stitch," she said with that faint hint of annoyance blended with affection.

"What? I've missed you Marisol and now that you're eating again, it reminds me how much I love your appetite." All of her appetites but I didn't want to go there. It was too soon. "Are you ready to talk?"

She froze and shook her head. "No, not now."

I couldn't deny that it hurt like hell that she didn't want to talk to me, but I also couldn't blame her. She'd been stuck with that bastard for a week of hell, probably unsure if I would keep my word to her. "Okay. But please, if you don't want to talk to me then talk to someone else. Moon is a good listener and she's all into that yoga and Zen shit that's supposed to help center you, or whatever. Please, babe?"

She grinned and slowly it spread and became the smile I'd seen on her beautiful face so many times. "You're a good man, Stitch."

"Don't sound so surprised, babe. I told you, I'm a catch." I patted my chest and a small laugh erupted out of her, making me feel about a thousand feet tall. But I was a good guy and I needed her to know that. "I want to help you, Marisol, in any way I can, but that doesn't mean we have to be together or sleep together if you don't want. I mean that."

I pushed back from the table and stood because what I had to say was important. "I like you, a lot, and I do want you, but if you don't want that, I'll still be here for you. You'll have to stay here until we're sure Carlito is gone but that's it."

I wanted her bad and hadn't realized it until Carlito had dragged her into that church basement, beaten and scared. But I couldn't be another man who wanted what she didn't want to give.

I wouldn't be *that* guy.

Ever.

She looked at me, her sad brown eyes trying their damnedest not to look it. I dropped back into my seat. Gutted. "Thank you, Stitch." She placed a hand on top of mine and I sighed at the warmth, the evidence she was coming back to life. "It's not that I don't want you, I'm just...I don't know, exhausted."

"Okay, I get it." That much I could deal with. "I'll sleep downstairs and have Jana and Moon check on you from time to time to make sure you're okay, yeah?"

She shook her head, eyes welling up with tears. "Can...can't you stay?"

Fuck yeah, I could stay. "If you want me to, Marisol, I'm here." When she looked at me this time, her whole face lit up and some of the color had come back. I had to fight the urge to crash my lips down on hers, but fuck me, I wanted to. "Whatever you need, babe."

She stood and rounded the table before she climbed on my lap and rested her head on my shoulder with her arms wrapped tight around me. "Right now, Stitch, I just need you to hold me."

So I did. I held on tight and let her soft curves lean into me. We sat like that for so long that my legs went numb and my ass began to tingle from being pressed into the scrawny wood kitchen chair but I didn't say a damn word. Not one fucking peep. I didn't move one inch unless Marisol needed to readjust. I may not have been the best bet for most of my life but right now she needed my warmth. My protection. My comfort. And I was damn well gonna give it to her.

That and so much more.

When she was ready.

Chapter Twenty-Six - Golden Boy

Two weeks had passed since the shit had gone down with the cartel. Lockdown ended and life was finally getting back to normal. Sort of. Everyone was still on high alert, including myself, but so far things had been quiet. Thanksgiving was right around the corner and I hoped to have a holiday without blood and without bullets. Without any fucking drama.

"Hey, Golden Boy, phone's ringing!" Lasso's voice pulled me from my thoughts that had interrupted the boring ass work of bookkeeping. Despite the money I'd gotten from my lawsuit against the State of Nevada, I ran a small business and that meant a lot of fucking paperwork. All of the fucking time.

"Yeah, I hear it," I grumbled and rubbed my eyes while the phone continued to ring. "Get Ink'd, what can I do for you today?"

"You can tell me what you're wearing, Tate." Teddy's husky voice was a purr over the phone, making me smile but when she used my given name, fuck that sound got me hot and ready to fuck.

"You first, Cover Girl." The silence on the line extended long enough to put me on edge. "What's up, babe?"

She sighed and I was already on my feet, scanning the office for my keys. "I need you to come home. Now."

I snatched the keys off the ring Jag had installed right by the door. "Is this a sex thing or something else?"

"Something else," she answered with a smile in her voice.

"I'll be there." I ended the call and went to the front where Jag stood at the counter, face buried behind a computer screen. "I need to head out. Something's up with Teddy."

Jag looked up. "Need a hand?"

"Don't know yet. I'll call if I do. You got things here?"

"Of course. Good luck."

The last time I got a call like this, Teddy's house had been set on fire. Then Jana had been shot and I got a call then too. I pushed my bike as fast as it would go until I pulled into our driveway and took the steps three at a time before bursting into the living room. "Teddy?"

"She's in the kitchen," Vivi said simply and I froze, looking from her to Katrina, who ran our Stetson Brothel. It was upscale, discreet and pricey. It was also our most profitable business other than weed. "Shit's happened but maybe your wife should fill you in."

"Why don't you fill me in?" I didn't mean to bark at Vivi but she would give me the facts only and that was what I wanted.

Straight up facts.

Vivi picked up the laptop she was working on and set it on the table, leaning back on the sofa and crossing her boot capped legs. "Kat's here because some strange fuckers have been coming into Stetson for the past few days. They're rough, which they pay for, but these guys are different, she says." She pointed at Kat who looked terrified. "Tell him."

She nodded, raking a hand through her hair before her eyes came back to mine. "Like she said, they pay for the rough stuff but Stetson isn't really the place for those kinds of guys, ya know?" I nodded because I did know. "But last night the Doc had to come because Bitsy got a fractured rib and Tawny's eye is swollen shut. I've never seen them before this week but a group of ten came in last night and Bitsy said her guy had a tattoo on his forearm. Double cursive S's."

"Salinas," Vivi confirmed.

"Shit." It was my turn to slid a hand through my hair and blow out a breath. "Why did you come here instead of the clubhouse?"

Vivi stood, wearing her badass uniform of black jeans and a matching black t-shirt with shit kicker black boots. "That's where I have to insist you talk to Teddy."

"I'm here." My wife entered the living room carrying a tray of drinks, looking as beautiful as ever. With the tray on the coffee table, she opened a beer and handed it to me, a true sign I wasn't gonna like what she had to say. "Some strange things have been happening at the office lately. At first I didn't think anything of it because, you know, shit happens." She smiled nervously and I grabbed her hand.

"Shit?"

She nodded and flicked her red hair behind her shoulders. "The power's been off since yesterday and then the plumbing went out. I asked Vivi to look into the building owner to see if he was trying to sell the building or raise rent or something. But when Kat came over today, I knew it was more."

"Shit, Teddy." I shook my head and stepped away from her, dialing Max to let him know what was going on before turning back to them. "Okay, why are you here again, Vivi?"

"Emotional support," she deadpanned.

"Tate," my wife called in a warning tone. "She's the one who saw that the power had been cut and the plumbing tampered with and she made me leave. When we got here, Katrina had just barely arrived."

Kat nodded, confirming my wife's version of events.

"There's nothing nefarious about my being here," Vivi said defensively, grabbing her laptop and her bag. "Now that you're here, I'm gone."

Dammit. "I never said that, Vivi."

"Doesn't matter," she muttered as she packed up her shit without looking at me. Or Teddy. Or Kat. She went to the door and held the knob. "It wasn't sophisticated, and they didn't break into the office to steal anything. Bolt cutters were used to cut the electricity and a good old fashioned rag to stop up the plumbing. It was just to scare you and maybe send a message," she said before yanking the door open and leaving before I could apologize.

"Jesus fuck, Tate. Can't you be nice to her after all she's done for us?" Teddy smacked me on the arms and chest about a dozen times in frustration.

"I didn't mean it how it sounded," I argued but it was no use, Teddy flew out the door to track down her friend and I turned to Kat.

"Anything else?"

"The girls are terrified and threatening to walk. I gave them the rest of the week off for the holiday." Kat was shaken and pale, terrified for her girls and probably herself.

"Thanks, Kat." The fucking cartel was a pain in my ass. "When Teddy comes back, tell her to pack a bag because we're all going back on lockdown to the club." She nodded and I turned to call Cross and fill him in on everything.

Again.

Fuck.

Chapter Twenty-Seven - Gunnar

The clubhouse was a fucking hive of activity when Lex and I got back from the store. As the designated gophers we were at the beck and call of Jana, Mandy and Kat, who were busy preparing for Thanksgiving. "Who in the hell starts cooking two days before the holiday?" I hefted two big ass turkeys onto the metal slab that Mandy insisted was a table but looked more like something you'd find at the morgue.

Jana turned to me with her hands on her hips and a gleam in her eye. "People who are cooking for a small army that includes at least a dozen men with hollow legs." Her arched blonde brows dared me to question her more but, wisely, I kept my mouth shut. "You didn't forget the hams did you, because we need ham."

"No, Jana, I didn't forget. But seriously, is all this necessary?"

Lex groaned as he dropped five canvas bags onto the floor beside the table. "A more important question is, is this everything you need to get through the holiday? The store was a fucking madhouse!"

Jana grinned. "The only upside to this lockdown is having someone else do the shopping." She turned and pulled two wrapped packages from the fridge. "Pastrami and mustard for you Lex and roast beef and horseradish for you Gunnar. Thanks for your shopping skills boys."

Lex grinned and stepped up to accept his sandwich, wrapping Jana in a one armed hug. "If this is my reward, all you have to do is ask Jana." He winked and vanished like he was afraid they might ask him to chop or peel something.

"You okay Gunnar? You look a little, I don't know, dazed."

That was part of it. "Just trying to make it through the day, same as everybody else." I grunted.

"Only it's different when you have a little one counting on you, right?" I nodded but kept quiet because I wasn't really the confiding type. "All you can do is enjoy the time you have. It could be a cartel or a drunk driver, you never know." Jana's lips twitched and I shook my head.

"You're not a very good motivational speaker," I told her, which only made her laugh.

"No, I'm not. I'm a realist and I also happen to be right."

"Yeah, thanks for the sandwich anyway." I left the kitchen before Jana tried to rope me into a conversation about my feelings because that shit wasn't happening. "Anyone seen Maisie?" There were kids everywhere, something that still surprised me every time I walked into the clubhouse. It wasn't all that long ago that we were all just a bunch of hard partying ex-military men who made money any way we could. Now, half the club was filled with family men.

What a difference a couple of years makes.

"She's outside." Black pointed to the rear exit where the playground had been set up and I frowned because it was too damn cold for any of the kids to be outside and it looked like Maisie was the only one.

Unease settled deep in my gut and I picked up my speed, pushing through the glass door that would take me to my sister. My kid. "Maisie!" The playground was empty but the sound of her familiar laughter sounded in the distance. "Maisie, where are you?"

"Here, Gunny!" I relaxed just a little at the sound of her happy tone and followed it. She knew better than to come out here alone so I hoped she had adult supervision. "Gunny!"

Around the giant slide I stopped dead in my tracks. Maisie stood with her little hands tucked into the pockets of her hot pink jacket, that Peaches woman next to her.

"What's going on back here?"

Maisie turned at the sound of my voice, her big blue eyes excited as she ran to me. "Peaches said girls can do anything." My sister who sounded more like an adult than I'd ever heard her sound, looked up at the woman for confirmation.

Peaches winked. "That's right, *Gunny*. Your sister said she likes cars."

That explained the giant race track that had been set up in the mulch at the free end of the play area. "Cars, huh?"

Maisie ran back to Peaches and grabbed her hand, nodding her head with more energy than I'd had in the last decade. "Fast cars," she clarified.

"I like fast cars," I insisted. Why in the hell I felt the need to justify my hobbies, I had no fucking clue, only that there was something about this Peaches woman that put me on edge. On the defensive.

"No one said you didn't. We were talking about Maisie." Peaches sent me an amused look like I was some jokester and that only pissed me off more. She ignored me and bent down with a hand on my sister's shoulder. "Okay Maze, this is the remote. Press it in the direction you want the car to go. Like this." She gave the excited little girl a quick lesson on remote control cars and then left her in control. "Ready?"

"Yeah!"

"Okay, then. Three, two, one...go!" Peaches stepped away, smiling as she watched my sister learn how to navigate the car. It took a few times before she got the hang of it but when she did, Maisie proved to be quite the speed demon.

A few times the car went off the track and I watched, amazed at how patient Peaches was with Maisie's exuberance. She exhausted me every single day and I wondered what motive Peaches had for being so kind. So nice to my little girl. "Oops. Sorry Peaches!" Maisie looked up at her with what I imagined were her best puppy dog eyes after she sent the car flying off the track and smacking against the leg of the slide.

Peaches looked down at her with wide eyes. "Holy crap Maze, did you see that? You made it flip like nine or ten times! How cool was that?" She laughed and whooped, loudly, until Maisie began to jump up and down excitedly.

"I did?"

"Yep. I think you're gonna be a stunt woman when you grow up, if the whole engineer thing doesn't work out."

"Engineer?" Maisie was almost three years old, there was no way in hell she even knew what an engineer was. "It's a little soon to be planning her future, don't you think?" Hell, I hadn't even started searching for a preschool or daycare center for her and she was *my* responsibility.

"I'm not planning anything, just enjoying some time with a fun little girl. Is that a problem?"

"Not as long as you remember that she isn't your little girl." I didn't need to bark at the woman, but I felt angry and frustrated and she was as good a target as any.

"Wow. Did you really just go there? You think I want to steal your kid?" Peaches huffed out a disbelieving laugh and shook her head before she dropped down to face Maisie. "I have to go take care of some boring grown up stuff, Maze. Enjoy the track, okay?"

"Do you hafta go, Peaches?"

She glared at me and nodded, giving Maisie a sad smile before she stood. "Apparently, I do, kid, but I want you to know that I had fun with you today. You're a cool little girl, stay that way."

"Okay, Peaches," she giggled, looking up at the woman with admiration shining in blue eyes so much like my own. "See you later."

"Later, Maze." She waved over her shoulder before turning to me with a glare. "Fuck you, Gunny." With a smirk she walked away, hips swaying to a beat that only I could hear. Dammit.

"Peaches, wait up!" She didn't stop and I looked back at Maisie, engrossed in trying to keep the car on the track. "Peaches, I'm sorry, okay?"

"Don't be. I know where I stand and I appreciate that." She stopped and turned to me so I could see that there was no anger there. Just resignation.

"Why are you being so nice to her?"

Peaches rolled her eyes. "She's a kid, why wouldn't I be? She wouldn't have any friends if the whole world judged her by her guardian."

That much was true and though I should have been grateful, I wasn't. "You don't even know her."

Peaches sighed heavily and took a step back. "You don't want me to spend time with your kid? Fine. I'll be gone soon enough anyway. Thanks for the warm fucking welcome, man."

I watched her walk away and yeah, I was an asshole with my eyes glued to her shapely ass until she disappeared from sight. "Shit!"

"Gunny said a bad word!"

A deep laugh sounded from behind me and I turned, ready to spring into action but it was just Jag.

"You scared the fuck out of me, Jag."

"Gunny said a bad word," Maisie said again, this time even louder.

I needed to watch my fucking words. "Maybe you were just too busy ogling Peaches to hear me. You were a real effin' dick, by the way."

"Tell me something I don't know."

Jag smiled and bent to pick up the car that once again fell off the track. He set it back in its place and grinned. "How about this…if Vivi gets wind of you bein' a dick, she might make it look like you never existed. Just so you know."

I barked out a laugh. Vivi was a crazy bitch but she had a lot of heart. For Jag and for the MC. "What are you doing out here?"

"Cross called church."

And just like that, my good mood faded. "What about?"

Jag gave me a look. "What do you think? Stetson is closed for the week but you saw Bitsy so you know what the fuck is going on. Apparently a few of the girls at the Bungalows had the same problems, which means *our* problems aren't as over as we thought."

"Goddammit! This ain't ever gonna end." Ever since I came back it was one shit show after another and I was pretty sure it wouldn't end until we were all dead.

"It will because we're gonna end it." Jag spoke with the kind of certainty I used to have when it came to the MC. But every year the other guys seemed to outnumber us, out gun us and worst of all, they were meaner than we were.

But we had no choice but to fight and to win. If we didn't, our women and children would face a worse fate. "If you say so, brother. Come on Maisie, we'll come back out later and play, okay?"

She looked up with pleading blue eyes. "Can Peaches come?"

I added *apologize to the sexy hacker* to the top of my to do list and nodded. "Anything for you, kid."

"Love you, Gunny!"

"Love you too, Maisie." Enough to do whatever it took to make sure the Reckless Bastards came out victorious against their latest enemies.

Chapter Twenty-Eight – Cross

Lying in bed with Moon nestled against my chest felt good. Hell, it felt damn good. This would be the first real holiday I'd spend with a woman other than Lauren. Instead of making me sad however, the thought brought a smile to my face. It had been a long road to recovery after I'd lost Lauren and the baby. Hard to forgive myself. Overcoming the guilt. And now I was living this, my second chance at life.

Moon woke up with a moan and a long stretch, her curves pressed up against me. "What's that smile for?"

Nothing better than waking up with my woman in my arms. A smile on her face and her hands roaming all over my body made sure most days got off to a great fucking start. "I was just thinking about Christmas. Beau. Lauren. And how lucky I am to have you."

"And what did you come up with?" That was what I loved most about Moon. She didn't shy away from the hard topics and talking about my dead wife never made her uncomfortable.

"I was thinking how proud she'd be that I finally moved on and found such an incredible woman. About how I'd thought I'd never love anyone as much as I loved her. Then came you." My statement was rewarded with a kiss. A slow passionate kiss that never failed to get me hard and aching for Moon. She was sensual in every sense of the word, from her graceful moves to the way she embraced pleasure and adventure.

"I think I'm the lucky one," she purred against me, dotting my jaw with kisses. "I am so thankful to have you in my life. You are a special man and I love you with all my heart."

Goddamn this woman had the power to bring me to my knees. If I wasn't already flat on my back with her womanly curves pressed on top of me, I would have been anyway. "Right back at you, babe. I love you more than I can say and I can't wait to make you my wife."

HOLIDAY HAVOC

Moon nipped my ear in that way she knew was guaranteed to drive me crazy. I thrust up against her until she threw her head back and moaned and ground against me. "As much as I want to make love to you right now, I'm on kitchen duty this morning." She smacked a kiss right over my heart. "As soon as you win against your latest big bad, we can set a date. Okay?"

"More than okay. Happy Thanksgiving, babe."

She smiled her beautiful, earthy, Zen woman smile that made my heart stutter and pushed off me, standing beside the bed in all her naked glory. "And happy Thanksgiving to you too, my love."

When Moon left me alone with my thoughts, I couldn't help but think of all the good things that had happened this year. Several brothers welcomed a new generation into the world, and some even added wives to the family. We all had something to live for, someone to fight for, which we needed because I had a feeling it would be necessary for the fight ahead.

I got dressed and stepped outside to inhale the cool morning air. Late November in Nevada could be hot as hell or cold as fuck but today the still chilly air felt good going down my lungs. I stepped back inside, bypassing my office and headed into the main area where the club mingled with the women and children playing games and setting the tables because according to Moon, this would be a typical Thanksgiving dinner where the meal was served just after noon to ensure everyone could eat nonstop. All day long.

"All right guys, we're whipping up some breakfast to tide you over until the big meal is done," Mandy shouted over the noise, her smile wide and her green eyes all business. "Someone bring in the coolers, please!" She clapped her hands a couple times, and just like that, several of the guys moved into action to do her bidding.

I grabbed up Dallas as he ran by, eager to help but too short to do anything helpful. "I gotcha little man. What do you think you're doing?"

"Helping!" His smile was big and toothy, looking so much like Lasso they could be twins.

"Let's help together." We gathered a stack of napkins and I handed each one to Dallas who then set it on top of a plate. We didn't stand on ceremony at the club so there was no point pretending with fancy napkin displays or holders.

Dallas and I were half finished adding napkins to the plates that Vivi's friend Peaches had set out, when a crash sounded outside. Since everyone was inside the compound with a few exceptions, I handed Dallas off to Rocky who wore a worried frown. "What's going on?"

"Don't know yet, Rocky. Keep the women and kids inside. Got it?" She nodded, leaving me free to head out to see what the fuck made that noise.

"Any idea what it could be?" Lasso asked, stopping right beside me and scanning the parking lot the same way I did.

"None." But then the culprit came into view. A red hatchback rolling down the driveway with flames coming out of all four windows. A busted up windshield with a brick through one side and most of the window missing on the other was headed straight for the light post. The cement light post. "Get a fire extinguisher! Now!" I didn't recognize the car but that didn't calm the icy dread from slithering into my blood and it had fuck all to do with the weather.

"What the fuck?" Savior ran outside, followed by Max, Jag, Stitch and Golden Boy.

"Do we know this car?" Jag looked around, his mind already spinning in about a thousand different directions.

Finally, the flaming heap came to a stop as it smashed into the light post with a sickening crash. For a long moment we all stood there, staring as the flames licked all around the car, a sick fascination passing through each of us, which said a lot because we were a jaded group of fuckers. Lasso came back, finally, with two fire extinguishers in his hands. "Let's get this fucking fire out before it spreads."

Golden Boy snatched one of the red cans from Lasso with a glare. "Let's get this shit over with, man." Without another word, Lasso and Golden Boy got to work killing the fire on all sides of the car. "Surprised they didn't set the fucking gas tank on fire."

"Is that a foot?" Lasso pointed to the backseat, eyes wide enough to tell me that it wasn't really a question.

"Fuck!" Savior kicked the back tire in anger. "It's a foot, a goddamn leg and a whole fucking body." His gaze slid to me, anger and questions burning there. He wanted to know what they all wanted to know.

What the fuck we were gonna do about this. "Any flames left?"

"Nah, it's out," Golden Boy assured me as he stepped back to make room so I could step closer.

A red and brown plaid blanket was draped over the body, covering everything but a woman's leg with a gold charm anklet melted onto her skin. She was white underneath the soot and the only other thing visible was a hand, shriveled and burnt. The door handle was too fucking hot to touch but I was too close now and I had a bad fucking feeling as I reached into the busted out window and pinched one end of the blanket and yanked it back. "Fuck!"

The woman was naked, and her body was well-preserved which told me the bastard who did this wanted us to recognize her. A few of the Reckless Bitches had shown up for Thanksgiving dinner so she might have been one of them but I didn't think so. The ankle that was protected from the fire showed signs of restraint with purple bruising all around it. Her wrists received the same treatment. "Whoever she was, they tortured her," Jag added, always the calm fucking voice of reason.

"Who is it?" Gunnar's gruff question echoed the sentiments of everyone around the still smoking vehicle.

I stepped closer as dread weaved its way around my body, squeezing so goddamn tight I was pretty sure I stopped breathing for nearly a minute, brushing brown hair, singed at the edges, away from the woman's face but even before I got there, I saw a very familiar tattoo. Tears burned my eyes and bile rose in my throat as I realized who it was.

"Fuck! Goddammit! It's Kat." We all knew that fucking tattoo, the pink heart with a peace sign inside of it, right there on her shoulder. Years ago when she'd been just a fast twenty year old trying to become an old lady, she used to prance around in next to nothing, that fucking tattoo on display.

"How do you know?" Savior moved in beside me and I grabbed his shoulder, knowing he would take her death—no her murder—the hardest. He'd always had a soft spot for Katrina, insisting he was no damn good for her but protecting her life all these years.

"That fucking tattoo right there," I told him and pointed at it.

"I will kill that little motherfucker with my bare hands!" Savior was so pissed off he radiated with it. The vein in his forehead stuck out dangerously and I knew it would be hard to keep him cool.

"Savior, go check on the women." He stayed where he was, staring at the lifeless body of Katrina. "Go. Now."

Max tugged him away from the car and shoved him inside the clubhouse, following just to be sure. The rest of the group remained in silent shock that one of our own had taken a hit.

"She was just at my house," Golden Boy said numbly. "Teddy will be devastated."

They would all be devastated. The wives and girlfriends didn't see Kat as a threat, they saw her as one of them. Family. I leaned back inside the car and brushed her hair away until I could see her face.

"Should we call the law?" Lex asked.

I shook my head. "Hell no. We can't. Kat would understand. Fuck!" It wasn't pretty. "Fuck!"

"What is it, Prez?" Stitch's voice was shaky. Worried and we all knew why. He felt responsible and he was worried that Marisol might meet the same fate if he let her out of his sight for one second.

"The bastard slit her throat from one end to the next." She was damn near decapitated. "Black eye. Bruises all over." Kat's wasn't the first body I'd seen or hell, it wasn't the first for any of us, but this one was deeply personal. As personal as any of the men and women we'd all lost on the battlefield. I kicked the side of the car as hard as I could. "Goddamn this fucking cartel!"

"I'm with Savior," Stitch growled. "We have to get this little motherfucker. We have to make them all pay for Kat."

"Especially that fat fuck Guapo," Gunnar said, his voice low and menacing. "I can't wait to fuck that asshole up!" He punched his palm a few times and we all knew what he had planned for Carlito's second in command.

I took a step back, away from the car. And then another step and another one until I could no longer smell the stench of Katrina's burning flesh. When I could finally take a breath without the smell of fire or smoke or seared skin, I sucked it in like it was fresh mountain air. Then I turned to face my men, feeling strong yet defeated, resolute. Resolved. "We can't just keep reacting to shit."

"We're not gonna respond?" Stitch was incredulous which was understandable, but respectful as always.

"Fuck yeah we are, but what we won't do is react. We need to come up with a solid plan so that we can go after this motherfucker and take him out for good. We must be smart and force him to react to us." What that plan was? I had no fucking clue, but I would.

Soon.

Jag nodded and clapped me on the back. "This is fucked up, man. Let's get everybody back inside and I'll grab a few prospects and clean this mess up. Kat was part of us and we gotta do this right."

I hated to leave Katrina out there, but Jag was right. It was time to set this shit aside and be thankful as fuck that most of us were still around to enjoy another holiday. I had no idea how we were going to handle this, but I knew flying off the handle was just what Carlito wanted. No, I needed to be smart and make sure something like this never happened to my family again.

Chapter Twenty-Nine - Jag

"Yo, Jag, did your girl find anything yet? It's been a few days and she hasn't said anything." Cross called out to me across the game room where a few of the guys had gathered, mostly to take a moment away from the serious shit of the past few days.

The women had been incredibly emotional after Katrina's body rolled into the compound. Some, like Vivi and Teddy had been more pissed and ready to kick some ass in their own right. I turned as Cross made his way to me. "Nah, man, I haven't heard a thing about it from her, but I'm headed to the camper right now." Vivi had been especially tight-lipped for the past few days but she'd been up late. Working. On what? I hadn't a clue.

"Find out and tell her time is a factor."

"She knows," I assured the Prez. "I'll get back with you soon," I promised.

"Good. And make sure she doesn't do anything stupid." I nodded and bit back a smile because I knew Cross didn't mean it the way it sounded, just that Vivi could be a bit impulsive and spontaneous. She never waited for the club's input when she thought she had a good idea.

"Got it." Cross clapped me on the back with a smile on his face as Moon and Beau walked through the front doors. I made my way to the camper, pulling the door open just as Peaches was getting ready to leave. "Hey Peaches. You ladies stirring up trouble?"

"Don't you know it, Jag. Problem?"

I nodded and held the door open for her. "Yeah. I'm pissed I wasn't invited along for the trouble."

Peaches laughed and Vivi joined in from somewhere inside the camper. "Yeah right," she called out. "My little Boy Scout doesn't do trouble."

Peaches and I exchanged a look before she jogged down the three steps and brushed past me. "Catch you lovebirds later."

HOLIDAY HAVOC

Vivi finally emerged, standing in the doorway looking hot as hell in black leather pants and a thin white tee shirt that clung only to her gorgeous tits. "What are you gonna do, hole up in your room for the rest of the night?"

Peaches shrugged. "Maybe. What the hell else am I gonna do?"

"Gunnar was giving you the eye," Vivi said with a knowing grin.

"Yeah, the stink eye. That guy hates me and thinks I'm gonna run off with his kid so yeah, I think I'll stay in my room until it's time to blow this joint."

"You're leaving?" Vivi looked distraught, a word I never would have ever attributed to her, at the thought of her friend leaving. "Where are you going?"

"I don't know, maybe back east or maybe I'll head to California. We'll see where the wind takes me."

Vivi crossed her arms and stared at her friend. "What's wrong with Vegas? Mayhem is pretty damn cool."

"I'll think about it."

"Liar." Vivi stepped down and got in Peaches' face. "Stay for the next few months and if you still hate it, I'll help you find a place and I'll come with you and set it all up." They engaged in a tense stand-off and I wasn't sure if it would end in a catfight or a make out session. Either would have been all right by me.

"Fine. Three months and no more."

Vivi grinned. "Perfect. Three months starting *after* we fuck up this cartel."

Peaches wanted to argue, it was written all over her face from the pinch of her bright lips to the way the skin between her eyebrows bunched up with annoyance. "Fine. But as soon as this is over, I get the camper."

"Deal!" I cut in because as soon as we were off lockdown Vivi was moving in with me. Without a fucking doubt.

Vivi and Peaches both turned to look at me, one with a question in her eyes and the other, a smile. "Oh yeah?" That was Vivi with a slinky look that made my cock twitch.

"Damn straight," I told them. "Cross wants to know what you got on Salinas?"

Peaches' eyebrows went up and disappeared behind her mane of curls and she took a step back. And then another. "What? I hear someone calling me, I'll uh, talk to you kids later."

"Vivi, is there something you want to tell me?"

"You look so handsome in that shirt." She traced a finger down the middle of my chest, tucking the tip inside my waistband. "So, so hot."

As much as I wanted to pull her inside the camper and slide deep inside her pussy, I knew she was hiding something. "Vivi, what did you do?"

She sighed, turned on her heels and disappeared inside the camper. "You're not gonna like it."

I had a feeling I would *more* than not like it. "Tell me anyway." I stepped into the camper and closed the door behind me, wishing I'd chosen to take her inside and fuck her like I wanted to. I had a feeling it would be a long time before we got to do that again. "Vivi."

"Fine. Sit down and don't say a word." I sat and listened to news I didn't like. Didn't fucking want to hear. News that made me so angry I didn't know whether to strangle her or tie her to the bed and fuck her. Hard. Fast.

"Grab your computer and let's go." Cross needed to hear this along with the rest of the MC. "You fucked up this time, Vivi."

"Again," she clarified. "I fucked up. Again. Only last time no one had a problem with me paying the price."

"Vivi," I called out to her but she didn't answer. A few minutes later she came back to what could loosely be called the living room with her sticker-covered laptop in her hand and a scowl on her face.

"Let's go." She brushed past me and kicked open the door before marching towards the clubhouse without a look back or another word.

Great. Vivi was surly enough on her own but when she was pissed off, like she was now, she could be a damn terror. By the time I caught up with her, she was leaning against the pool table with her laptop open and her eyes glued to the screen.

"I'll get everyone together."

"Great," she snarled into her screen.

Fifteen minutes later, Cross had gathered the whole MC into the game room because women still weren't allowed in the Merry Mayhem room. "All right, Vivi what do you have for us?"

She took a deep breath and stared, raking her fingers through her hot pink hair as she stood and fixed her eyes on the silver Mayhem skull, dotted with onyx and ruby. "I've been doing some digging into Salinas and into Carlito specifically and it turns out that the guy isn't all that sophisticated. He had or has dozens of mortgages on his homes, from his lavish villa in Tamaulipas to a bunch of shitty little houses that were clearly stash houses."

"You got addresses for those stash houses?" Teddy looked around until her gaze landed on Golden Boy.

"I do."

"And?" Cross was losing his patience with her slow drip of information.

"And," she sighed impatiently. "I sold three of the addresses to the *Familia De La Muerte* cartel." She stood there with her back straight and her shoulders squared, ready to take on whatever bullshit the guys flung at her.

"You did *what*?" Cross stood with his arms folded over his chest, blue eyes glaring at Vivi.

"You heard me. They murdered Kat and the *Familia De La Muerte* are in a position to do something about it. You guys are not. I'm sorry if that hurts your feelings but it's a fact. You can't take these guys on."

"What the fuck do you mean you *sold* them?" Gunnar was on his feet, an angry glare on his face and murder in his eyes. It took everything I had not to stand up and protect my girl, but I knew she could handle it.

She'd want to handle it and would probably kick my ass if I tried to intervene. "What part of that is unclear, Gunnar?"

Angry, Gunnar took a step forward and then I did intervene. "Watch yourself, man."

"You heard what she said, Jag. You're seriously gonna take her side?"

"Jesus fuck!" Vivi growled and tossed a cue ball across the room, the loud crack against the concrete wall shut everyone up. "Yeah I get it, you're pissed that I did this without talking to you but guess what? I don't fucking answer to you. Not any of you," she said, letting her angry glare linger on me a little longer than everyone else. "You don't have the man or firepower to fight a cartel and you damn well know it," she told Cross, so damn confident in her convictions that a few of the guys sat down, more intrigued than angry now.

"That's our choice to make," Cross insisted. "Not yours."

Vivi nodded and folded her arms across her chest, feet crossed at the ankles as she leaned against the pool table. "And I haven't taken that away from you. I exacted a bit of my own revenge because I liked Kat and I don't fucking like anyone."

"And when Carlito retaliates?" Golden Boy asked, his face impassive and his tone even, which surprised me.

"On who? Us or the *Familia De La Muerte*? Look," she groaned and pinched the bridge of her nose. "When Carlito's stash houses are hit, they'll kill a few of his guys, steal his product and burn that place to the ground. That means he loses money and men, the two things that keep him feeling like a big fucking deal. Without them—"

"Without them he'll come after us and our families, or don't you give a shit about that?" Cross interrupted.

"You mean the way he came after Katrina when you did absolutely fucking nothing? Get real if you think there's anything you can do to end this without violence. When he starts losing men and money, Carlito will become desperate and that's when he'll fuck up and make a mistake."

"That tiny motherfucker is cocky as shit," Stitch said, agreeing with her, another surprising move since we were all pretty sure he was still targeting the Bastards because of Marisol.

"But killing a dozen men won't do shit," Savior grunted angrily.

Vivi blew out a breath. "You know this isn't my first rodeo. And if you guys think it'll stop with the stash houses, you're naïve as fuck. *Familia De La Muerte* wants Salinas territory, they always do, which means they'll keep going without us. Salinas will be fighting two enemies. At least."

Damn, my girl was sexy as hell when she was being an evil criminal mastermind. Her plan was well thought out and even though it wasn't what I would have done, it did have plenty of merit. "Okay so what else do we need to know?"

"Watch the news, there have been at least a dozen deaths in and around Tamaulipas, and that's just in the past twenty four hours." With a disgusted snort, Vivi slammed her laptop shut and stared at my group of brothers.

"Maybe your plan does have some solid points," Gunnar conceded, "but it wasn't your plan to execute."

"That's where you're wrong, Gunnar. I do what I do and when your club needs help, I provide it. I don't work for you and I don't fucking answer to you. You don't like how I choose to handle my shit? Too damn bad." She snatched up her laptop and sent a hurt glare my way. "You know what? Do it your way, I don't give a shit. I guess you'd rather plan the battle than win the war." She stomped off, muttering about idiotic men with egos bigger than their cocks.

"What the fuck, Jag?"

I glared at Gunnar, ready for a goddamn fight after listening to my brothers tear into my woman. "What's the matter, Gunnar? Pissed off you didn't think of it first?"

"Come the fuck on, guys!" Stitch clapped his hands loudly and grinned. "That was a genius fucking plan. Now Carlito has to fight us on this side of the border and the *Familia* on his home turf. That can only spell good things for us."

"Of course you'd say that," Gunnar snorted. "You want him dead before he comes after your ol' lady and we all know it."

"Settle the fuck down!" Cross roared. "I don't have to like it but what Vivi did was good thinking. It gives us just the edge we need to get a leg up on this asshole."

"And I think you'd all show a little fucking gratitude given the hit Vivi took for us," I reminded them. Again. I didn't like watching them go after her like that and even though I knew that no woman was more capable than my woman, it still left a bad taste in my mouth.

"How long are you gonna milk that for, Jag?"

I turned to Golden Boy and frowned. "Until every one of you mother fuckers remember that she could have said no. The feds could have locked us all up for a lot longer than they did her. I'm not saying give her special treatment, but like Vivi said, she doesn't work for us."

"That's bullshit—" Gunnar began but Cross cut him off.

"That's enough. We have some planning to do so everyone to Merry Mayhem in five minutes."

Chapter Thirty - Stitch

"Are you gonna be okay?" Marisol had just started to get some color back in her skin and she was just starting to talk and smile a little bit more. And then Kat was murdered. Horrifically so and ever since, she'd been quiet as hell. No, not quiet, silent. "Please, Marisol, say something. I have club shit to deal with today but I need to know you'll be okay while I'm gone."

I never understood what could make a man want to take a bullet for a chick, or to give up the endless supply of pussy on offer when girls found out I was in a biker club. But now, I kind of got it. I wasn't in love with her or anything like that, but I did give a shit about her.

Marisol stared at me, her big brown eyes lifeless. The spark that usually lit up her whole damn face, extinguished. And it was all Carlito's fault. It may not bring her spark back, but I would make him pay for that. She shrugged, like it didn't matter if she'd be okay or not. She gave a short nod before turning her gaze out the window.

"Marisol." My voice came out low, guttural as I cupped her face to make her look at me. "Please, babe, I need you to show me some signs of life. I need to take care of business but I won't be able to if I'm worried about you."

"I'm fine, Stitch. Really. Go do whatever it is you need to do." Then she sat up and held my face in her hands like I was more than her protector. More than someone she used to fuck. "Just be careful. Enough people have died because of me."

"Not *because* of you, Marisol. Because of that fucking psycho and believe me babe, as soon as I get the fucking chance, he's a dead man."

Her lips twitched into a sad smile. "Be careful, Stitch. I won't ask what you have to do because I don't want to know, but I do want you to come back safe."

"Aww shit, girl, you do care." She smacked my arm and that show of life, that smile, pulled a laugh from me. "Don't worry about me, I'll be fine."

Her eyes said she thought I was full of shit, but Marisol nodded anyway and stood, smoothing the plain green shirt down, which hung loose because she'd been eating like a damn bird. "And don't worry about me, Stitch." To prove her point, Marisol went to the door of the small apartment and opened it.

She left before I could get my boots on and go after her, but when I caught up with her, she had just stepped into the kitchen where Jana wrapped her into a big, welcoming hug. "Marisol, it's so good to see you! How are you doing?"

"I've been better, Jana. But it smells amazing in here. How can I help?"

Jana looked thrilled by Marisol's change, but I was as suspicious as I was surprised. She'd been a goddamn mute for the past few days and now she was offering to help? "We're putting together some more leftovers but we're being creative about it so grab an apron and a cutting board. There's some dark meat over there with your name on it."

Marisol looked over at me, brows arched as if to say, "See, I'm fine." And even though I was still skeptical as hell, she seemed all right. Plus, I knew Jana would mother the hell out of her until she was fine for real. "See you later, ladies."

"Be careful," Marisol called out to me just before I left the kitchen, making me smile to hear signs of life from her. She'd been through a fuck ton of shit lately and I knew it would take some time before things—before *she*—got back to normal, but I couldn't help but want to speed that shit up.

"Hey man." I was so goddamn lost in thought that I didn't see Gunnar until he was right in front of me.

"What's up Gunnar?" He was the last fucking person I wanted to talk to, but he was my brother and that was the only reason I didn't punch his fucking lights out.

"How's it, uh, going?" Gunnar looked nervous, which I didn't even think he could feel, but it didn't make shit between us right.

"Fine. Did you want something?"

"Nothing, just…fuck man, I'm sorry about—"

I cut him off because I didn't want to hear his goddamn excuses. "Don't worry about it, Gunnar. We've got shit to take care of right now and honestly I don't fucking believe you anyway."

"Maybe I deserve that but it's true. I am sorry and I know none of this shit is your fault."

"Right," I snorted and spotted Cross headed our way. "What's up, Prez?"

"I just got a delivery. A fucking phone." He held up the phone, obviously a burner and an old fucking one at that. "Come on."

Gunnar and I followed him into Merry Mayhem where the rest of the club was already waiting. "Carlito?"

"That's my guess," Cross said as he flipped open the phone and played the voicemail. A heavily accent, slightly nasally voice sounded and it was a voice I knew all too well. Gunnar too. A voice neither of us was likely to forget.

"All right Mr. Cross, you have my attention. And now that you do, you might not want it. You have fucked with me and now I intend to fuck you back."

The room fell silent as the gravity of Carlito's words sank in.

The fight was on.

Chapter Thirty-One - Max

Waking up with Jana in my arms was the best damn part of my day and today that was especially true. Her curves, softer now since the birth of our babies, pressed up against me, teasing and tempting me awake. With a low groan as she stretched and smiled up at me, her green eyes opening with a sparkle. "Have a good sleep?"

I nodded because every night with her cuddled up beside me was a good one. Jana was my own personal dream chaser, unknowingly slaying the nightmares that sometimes still made sleep difficult. "Yeah." It wasn't the most satisfying sleep because today wasn't going to be an easy day. Not by a fucking long shot. But, I was ready for it. Battle ready. "Better with you right here."

Her skin flushed and she propped her head up on her hand. "I'm glad."

Just those two words were all I needed to hear from my wife to settle my mind and focus on the day ahead. All of the whore houses were closed today aside from the private, invitation-only ones that no one knew about and those who did were too afraid of the consequences to talk. That didn't change the fact that we had to make sure our girls were safe. All of them. They were under our protection but they also made up a big chunk of our income, so security was tight everywhere, from the weed shops to the brothels as well as all of our personal holdings. Carlito was a crazy motherfucker and we didn't put anything past him. "How'd you sleep, babe?"

Jana's smile brightened and I felt it all the way down to my bones. This woman, this petite little blonde who'd taken my life by storm and made me whole, was my rock.

She climbed on top of me, her knees bracketing my hips as she leaned forward to cup my face. "I love you Max. I love the hell out of you and I know you're gonna come back to me because it took me too damn long to find you." She smashed her lips to mine in a forceful kiss that stole my breath and got me hard in one second flat. She slipped her tongue inside my mouth and deepened the kiss until I was ready to plunge into her and forget that today might be the day I lost another one of my brothers.

Too damn soon, she pulled back with a kind smile. "Now go out there and kill those motherfuckers. Do it for Kat. Do it for Marisol. And do it because I'm telling you that it's okay." She cupped my face with an intense look on her face. "I'm telling you, Max, to unleash that part of you that you think you have to keep from me, from all of us. Let that guy out to rip these fuckers apart and make them regret they ever fucked with the Reckless Bastards."

My smile was so damn big I was pretty sure my face was gonna split right there with my girl on top of me, gently grinding into me just in case I forgot what I had waiting for me back at home. "You're so hot when you get bloodthirsty, babe." Then I grabbed her ass and pulled her down against my cock and kissed the hell out of her, making sure she knew exactly how much she meant to me. How dedicated I was to making sure I wrapped her in my arms tonight.

After bringing my wife to a quick orgasm, I slipped from the bed and looked at her, splayed out and naked with a satisfied smile on her face. "I expect you right beside me tonight when I go to sleep."

"Where else would I be?" Her laugh sounded behind me as I left the room to hug and kiss my kids before I went downstairs to the clubhouse. To strap up.

That was the thing about being a military man, no matter what branch you were in, the readiness never disappeared. It came right back, just like riding a bike.

I strapped a gun to each of my ankles, back up pieces to go along with the one at my side and tucked into a holster at the back of my jeans. I added a few knives for good measure because when I went to war, I did whatever I had to in order to survive. There were no rules of engagement, not when the enemy didn't follow the same rules, and this wasn't a sanctioned sport. I had to survive any way I could.

End of story.

When I was strapped up, I joined the guys and Vivi in the main room, walking through a big ass cloud of cigarette smoke to get there. "We good to go?"

Vivi nodded, her sarcastic wit just the thing we all needed to keep us focused on what we had to do. "As long you're ready to deep fry a cartel boss, sure." A few of the guys laughed and she rolled her eyes, still not quite ready to forgive any of us for our display last week.

"Anyway, Carlito is on the move, about ten miles from the meeting spot."

"You sure, 'cause we're not supposed to meet for another five hours." Cross' expression mirrored what we were all thinking, at least what I was thinking.

"Ambush," Golden Boy and Savior said at the same time.

"Probably." Cross raked a hand through his hair in stress and blew out a frustrated breath. "Goddammit!" He was on the brink of a tirade but the appearance of Vivi's friend Peaches, curves on display, halted it.

Thankfully.

"Okay boys, Vivi said you might need some comms and a contact of mine came through spectacularly. We got some top of the line radios with a fifty-mile radius and unless there's a military or police operation going on in the vicinity, you should have zero interference."

"What the hell do we need comms for?" Gunnar was as gruff as he always was, but he seemed to be even worse when it came to Peaches.

She looked at him, brows raised and amusement shining in her eyes. "So that you can communicate, obviously. Now put them in and test them out so we can get the kinks out before you bounce."

Vivi leaned back in her chair and kicked her booted feet up on the card table with a grin. "And all you mother fuckin' angels can just call me Charlie."

At least *she* thought it was funny.

Chapter Thirty-Two - Jag

"We need to be ready for anything. I don't trust this fucker as far as I can throw his little ass." Cross stayed on his bike with me right beside him, eyes focused below us about two clicks ahead where Carlito stood beside a flashy white Escalade because heaven forbid the dumbass kept a low profile.

"Me either, but he won't do anything too stupid without his enforcer." Guys like Carlito were all the same, strong and crazy as long as they had stronger and crazier backup. On his own, he was mostly talk.

"How sure are you that Guapo's gonna show up at the clubhouse?" Cross asked.

"He doesn't need to be sure, boss man, because I'm sure," Vivi cut in on our conversation, something I was sure Cross had forgotten about based on the frown he wore. "The tracker on his bike says he's on his way here now."

At Vivi's words, tension coiled in my gut. I knew she could take care of herself, could handle a knife and a gun as well as she could a computer, but I also knew Guapo was a crazy motherfucker. He'd killed people just for the fun of it and he enjoyed it. The guy was unhinged and he was heading Vivi's way. "Be careful," I told her.

"Always am, babe. Always am." Vivi was always careful, except when she wasn't. "Guapo's ETA is about five minutes."

Cross nodded, his jaw tight with tension. "Guys, you hear that?"

"Yeah, boss. We hear you." Savior barked into the comms, pissed off that he'd been picked to stay back with Black and keep the compound safe.

"Good. Stitch, you en route?"

"Yep, just rounding Skull Rock now."

Cross gave me a look and I started my bike, leaving the meeting spot, at least as far as Carlito was concerned. About two miles from the meeting point, I stopped my bike and climbed up the side of Skull Rock where Stitch left my rifle. "In place."

"Good. Stay alert."

There was still an hour until the meeting time and we were in no more a hurry than Carlito was to start early, he just didn't know why. But we did. "Guapo is in the building," Vivi said sharply and I was on edge, hating that I couldn't be there with her. To protect her.

All I could do was listen. Even though I wasn't there, I knew the plan because we'd gone over it a dozen times. Mostly for my own peace of mind. Vivi would be standing at the bar like she was nothing more than one of the Reckless Bitches, her laptop behind the bar, a gun under her leather jacket and a comm in her left ear, where her pink hair would shield it from discovery. If it came to that.

"Can I help you? This is private property and I don't know you." That meant Guapo was inside.

"You could know me. We could be friends, *chica*."

Vivi laughed flirtatiously, something she'd had Peaches coach her on because my woman did not subscribe to the whole *catch more bees with honey* school of thought. "Yeah? How about you, me and Billie Jean be friends?"

"Billie Jean? Sounds kinky," Guapo said, a smile in his voice that I knew he would soon regret.

The sound of the shotgun cocking came through loud and clear. "Billie Jean wants to go first. Ah, ah...not so fast asshole. State your business before Billie Jean gets to your dick first."

"Easy, *chiquita*. I'm just looking for a friend of mine, Marisol Luna."

"I'm not your *chiquita* and I've never heard of her."

"She's been here for weeks. Maybe you don't know everyone around here?" He was taunting her, probably thinking she was nothing more than a piece of biker ass.

"I know everyone who matters and if your friend is a biker bunny, then she ain't worth knowin' and she ain't here. If I was you, I'd get going before things get uglier than your mug."

"Mouthy bitch," he grunted. I swore it took everything within me to stay up on that rock with my gun aimed at Carlito's head, just in case shit went sideways.

Vivi laughed. She fucking laughed like this was all some joke. "I've been called worse, Guapo."

"You know me?" He sounded confused. Vivi must have nodded because Guapo kept talking. "Then you know I'm not some one you want to fuck with."

"Oh, I don't know, Mr. Guapo. I heard Gunnar took you out pretty easily, twice, and that guy is all talk." She laughed at what I could only assume was an incredulous look from Guapo.

"I can hear you," Gunnar grumbled which only produced more laughter from Vivi.

"Just give up Marisol and this will all be over. *El Jefe* won't stop until he has her back."

Vivi sighed and I could hear the sound of the shotgun being set on the bar. "How well do you know your *Jefe*? I mean *really* know him?"

"We have known each other since we were children. *Mi padre* raised him like he was his own." The emotion in Guapo's voice paid true to Vivi's theory about the enforcer.

"Yes, Cadre, right? Funny thing about the way he died, right? A late night car explosion after visiting his mistress, something less than a handful of people knew about."

"*Felicidades.* So you use Google."

Vivi laughed again. "Google, that's cute. But you know what Google didn't tell me? That the police captain down in Tamaulipas, Captain Martinez, confirmed what even you probably suspected. Carlito was behind the bomb in your *padre's* car."

"Liar!"

HOLIDAY HAVOC

"You wish I was lying because you know what this means. What you have to do, but I'd just as soon have the Reckless Bastards kill you all. I'm just saying I'd be pretty fucking pissed off if I'd been playing servant and errand boy to the man who put a bomb under my dad's car just so he could take over the cartel, which technically speaking, should be yours."

Guapo barked out a laugh. "And I'm just supposed to believe you, some whore to a motorcycle gang?"

"I don't give a shit what you believe. What I know is that I spoke to Martinez myself, at his gorgeous estate in Montecito. You know where that is? It's where Oprah lives, pretty swanky digs. I wonder where he got the cash." Vivi did an excellent job of playing this fool and I couldn't wait to show her how proud I was.

"A dirty cop in Mexico is no surprise."

"Maybe not, but it got me to thinking. Martinez was a young guy when he left Mexico, barely forty so how did he accumulate so much cash in so little time? I did some digging though, well a lot of digging because that's kind of my thing. I'm just a club whore on the side, you see," she rambled briefly. "This is what I really do."

There was silence for a long time and then an audible pained groan. "You forged this," Guapo accused. She must have given him the papers we'd discussed earlier.

"Nope. This is straight from the bank. I even left the routing numbers visible because I wouldn't expect a professional sadist to take my word for it. And before you even ask, yeah, that's a number to one of the Salinas accounts." Vivi took a deep breath and from the sound of it, she must have set the small tape recorder on the bar and hit play.

"Everyone knew it was Carlito because he came into the station, just sixteen years old, with a picnic basket full of cash and one request. Make the bombing look like it was the job of another cartel. So we did. We killed one of the Aztecas Negros foot soldiers and put his fingerprints on what was left of the bomb. He was dead and everyone bought the story."

"Turn it off!" Guapo was good and riled up now. Emotional. And my girl was alone with him. There was another long, tense silence before he spoke again. "You are sure about this?"

"Yeah, I'm sure. The last deposit was just ten days ago. Every two weeks for the past nineteen years."

"Aaaah!" The sound from Guapo was visceral, the rage palpable. "If you are lying, if this is some ploy, I will come back and skin you alive *chica*."

Knowing Vivi, she grinned at his threat. "I look forward to it, Guapo. And I don't need to make this shit up because it's the truth. Yeah, it helps us but I imagine it helps you more."

"I mean it *chica*."

"I look forward to it, Arturo." A deep chuckle sounded and seconds later, Vivi let out a loud breath. "He's gone and he's pissed."

"We all heard, babe. Great job."

"Yeah, thanks. Stay safe boys, Guapo is moving toward the meeting point at a fast clip. He'll be there in less than fifteen."

"Thank you, Vivi."

I wondered if it cost Cross anything to say those words. I knew my guys were no fans of such a headstrong woman but this would make the second time Vivi saved our asses. I hoped they appreciated it.

"Thank me by bringing my old man back in one piece. Good luck."

I hoped like hell we didn't need luck.

Chapter Thirty-Three-Cross

Five minutes. That's how long until the clock struck three and we'd come face to face with the crazy motherfucker who'd made my life hell when I should have been enjoying this holiday season with my woman. My boy.

"You gonna be cool, Stitch?"

I knew he, more than the rest of us, wanted Carlito dead because of what he'd done to Marisol, but this would only work if the new patch kept his cool.

Stitch gave a crisp nod, fingering his stubble anxiously. "I'll be cool. Marisol is safe but if Guapo doesn't kill that fucker, he's mine."

"Fair enough." Three minutes left. "Ready?"

Stitch nodded again, the muscles in his jaws clenching with the effort to remain cool. "Everybody, give me a quick radio check." One by one the members of the Reckless Bastards checked in with a go call. "All right, let's do this shit." We rode side by side, stopping with only about twenty feet between us and Carlito's pearly white SUV, where he stood with three men, armed with AK-47 assault rifles.

We'd picked this spot because it was a perfect place for an ambush. The terrain was covered with boulders big enough to hide a tank, or in this case, several heavily armed Reckless Bastards hidden around the rocks waiting for the call or shit to hit the fan.

"Cross, so good to see you *mi amigo*." He wore a big toothy grin, greeting me like we were old buddies and not two men looking for the first opportunity to kill the other.

"We ain't fucking amigos asshole, unless you regularly kill the employees of your friends." I could've put a bullet through him for Katrina alone, never mind what he put my club through. The unnecessary worry he put Moon through.

"That was just a preview of things to come." Carlito waved his hands dismissively as if slicing a woman's throat was no big deal but it was—it was a huge fucking deal. He smirked and I wanted to smack that look off his face. "Lesson learned, right?"

I scoffed. "I guess we'll see about that, won't we?"

He nodded and took a few steps forward that separated himself from his men, but still kept a few feet distance to us. "Let's talk business, Cross. I have a proposition for you. I don't think you will want to turn it down." His tone was arrogant, like he could force me to say yes. "Be my top distributor in America. Funnel the shipments for me before they move across North America."

I laughed at that. "We don't fuck with drugs."

"Too bad," he said, much too easily which was just another piece of evidence that he was wasting time and he had no idea it was a pointless gesture. "Looking for someone, Carlito?" Guapo should have been at his side by now and he was getting worried.

"No." He gave a flick of his wrists and the three black SUVs that had been waiting about a half mile away, pulled up behind him. "I have everything I need."

All four doors of each car opened, revealing four armed men, all of them carrying AK-47's.

"Doesn't look much like a friendly chat now, does it?" At his smile I crossed my arms to show that asshole that I wasn't worried. Although to be honest, I had no idea why this asshole and his goons hadn't tried to blow us away already. "I mean, it's just me and Stitch here, yet you've got all these armed men. Plus, I'm sure your enforcer is around here somewhere too."

Carlito tossed his head back and laughed way too hard at something that wasn't all that funny. "I thought you were a better businessman Cross, or at least a better *gangster*."

Under normal circumstances he would have been right, but the problem with guys like Carlito was that they never looked past the big, flashy move to see the subtle moves that were ten times more effective.

"You know, Carlito, sometimes it pays to be smarter, not better."

That wiped that smarmy fucking grin off his face but the high pitch wheeze of one of those racing bikes sounded in the distance and his smile returned. "Too bad you weren't smarter *and* better. Things could have gone differently."

Guapo pulled up, parking his bike between me, Stitch and Carlito. He spared a quick, blank, look at me and Stitch before turning to Carlito. He gave him a head nod. "*Jefe.*"

"Things taken care of?"

"*Si,*" he answered in Spanish.

Carlito's smile broadened. "Sorry about your girl, Stitch," he called out, too damn arrogant for the reality of the situation. "I will punish her, dearly, but you can rest easily because I will not kill her. No. I will put Marisol to work in one of my *casitas*. Perhaps the little whore will work in Tijuana."

Stitch grinned with his arms crossed. Looking much too casual for the news he'd just received. "Sure about that, are you?" He scoffed.

I saw the flicker of doubt and worry in his eyes. "I have no reason to worry, do I, Guapo?"

Judging by Guapo's stance, arms crossed with his shoulders broad and an angry look on his face, Carlito had every reason to worry. "I want to talk about Cadre," Guapo growled out.

He hid it well, but another flicker of worry crossed Carlito's face. "Don't be stupid, Guapo. We can talk about this later, right now we have business."

"No. We will talk about it now. This has everything to do with business." Guapo took a step forward and Carlito took a step back. I couldn't help but smile at how well the plan was playing out.

"I don't know what you are talking about."

"*Mi padre,* did you kill him, Carlito, yes or no?"

"Guapo, *por favor—*"

"Yes or no, goddammit!" He held up a silver handgun with a glossy wood finish and aimed it at his employer. "Answer me!"

"You want an answer?" Guapo's only response was to pull back the safety and wrap his finger around the trigger. "Okay, I'll give you an answer. Yes, I killed him. He was in my way, standing where I should have been standing. What was I supposed to do?"

"You killed my father." Guapo bit out. Both men glared at each other. "You killed my father! *Mi padre!*" His voice broke on the last word and I reached behind me where I kept my favorite piece because shit was about to explode.

Carlito laughed at his cousin's display of emotion which only pissed him off. Guapo ran full speed at Carlito, knocking him to the ground with his knees pressing into the other man's arms, effectively pinning him to the ground. Both hands raised in the air, Guapo rained fists down on his cousin's face until blood flew from his fists, rage and anguish propelled him forward, pushed him to land blow after blow.

"Guapo!" Carlito screamed, terror and pain squeezing the breath out of him. *"Por favor."*

"*Now* you say please, when your life is on the line?" Guapo spit at the man and stood, which was a mistake because Carlito pulled out a small gold gun with a white handle and squeezed the trigger, sending Guapo to the ground.

"You should have killed me when you had the chance, *Primo*." Carlito turned to me with a sly grin. "Kill them all," he ordered his men as he pulled himself up off of the ground.

Stich went straight at Carlito and knocked the fancy gold gun away and then I kicked Carlito square in the jaw sending his face crashing back into the desert sand. Stich and I took an arm and dragged Carlito toward the boulder next to our bikes. We used him as a human shield as my boys rained down hell fire on his countless men with automatic weapons.

"Shit!" I spared a glance at Stitch who smiled like he was on a goddamn roller coaster. He kept Carlito pinned down with one knee. I could tell Carlito was wearing a vest, but he was bleeding from two places that I could see. Clearly those bullets were meant for me and Stitch.

More bullets flew, a high-pitched whine sounded three times and then Jag's voice came over the comms. "Got three down. Nope—make that four."

"Where the fuck are they coming from?" I asked over the comms.

"You're surrounded, but we got you covered." Jag replied.

Our odds were getting better by the second. Stitch and I shared a look at Carlito and knew he wasn't going anywhere fast. I took a deep breath and checked my weapons. I had US Military grade M-16 semi-automatic rifle strapped over my shoulder with a 50-round clip cartridge, locked and loaded. I also had a Glock 9 in each hand with 20 round clips each.

Stitch and I both emerged from opposite sides of the rock with guns blazing. I dropped one of Carlito's men, who was making his way toward our left flank with another guy, on the third shot. When the first guy fell, the second guy hesitated just long enough for me to sink two shots into him center mass that sent him flying into the fender of one of the SUV's.

"Fuck!" A shot ripped through my left shoulder. I could feel the burn and I gritted my teeth and pulled back behind the rock to check myself out. Luckily it was just a flesh wound and I quickly moved around to the other side of the rock to see how Stitch was doing.

"You all right Prez?"

"Yeah." I nodded at Stitch who was shooting like a madman. "I'll live. These motherfuckers are coming out of the fucking woodwork! Just keep shooting." I looked down and saw two empty clips next to him. That crazy fucking kid had already unloaded two clips and had taken out at least three of Carlito's men while the rest of our brothers had the bad guys surrounded.

Jag had taken care of most of them, but Golden Boy and Lex were holding their own. And Lex didn't fuck around. He had a fully automatic weapon that I didn't even bother to question where he got it. And I wouldn't.

I looked over at Golden Boy just as he took a bullet to the side, he looked okay and managed to take out the asshole before he fell to the ground with a grunt. "I'm hit, I'm hit!" he called out over the comms, Vivi quickly broke in.

"Get your fucking asses back here and we'll have a doctor waiting."

"I'm out of ammo," Gunnar yelled and ran toward a big fucking dude with no neck. He took a fist to the face but that was it as his big body fell against the bigger man.

Gunnar grabbed him by his head and slammed it against a small rock sticking out of the ground. He kept going, over and over and over again, until he was more than sure that he'd finished him off for good.

"You'll have a hell of a shiner Gunny, but hey chicks dig scars right?" Jag's voice sounded through the comms, pure amusement. "One more left, who wants 'em?"

"Already got 'em," Max said, seconds after a final shot rang out. "Too slow, Jeremiah."

Jag groaned into the comms at Max's use of his given name. "Yeah, good job old man."

Stitch nodded towards the rock where we'd left Carlito bleeding out. "He's mine now, right Prez?" I knew Stitch was eager to kill Carlito and I nodded.

"Yeah, go ahead."

I followed close behind as he rounded the big rock. "Hey Carlito, you fucking prick!" Carlito was still very much alive and apparently had another piece because he took a shot at Stitch as he rounded the corner. The bullet missed its mark and only grazed Stitch on the neck.

Stitch kicked the gun out of his hand, sending it flying. "You shoot like a bitch, asshole!" Stitch wiped his free hand on his fresh wound and smiled at Carlito squeezing the trigger twice, sending two bullets straight into the little fucker. One hit him in the groin and another under his arm.

Two red dots grew into bigger vibrant red blotches against the dirty white suit. Carlito looked down in disbelief at the pool of blood oozing out of his wounds as if the fucker actually thought he'd never get shot. "I still have Marisol and you need me alive to ever see her again."

"Actually you don't motherfucker." Stitch said, still holding his neck. "She's right in my bed where she belongs."

"Are you sure?"

Stitch nodded, his smile wide and satisfied, his arm extended with the gun pointing right at Carlito. "Doesn't matter, right? You're a dead motherfucker."

A shot rang out from behind us that made half of Carlito's head explode. Stitch and I turned to see Guapo standing there with his piece aimed at Carlito.

"Guapo." I gave him a slight nod. Stitch helped me to my feet, removing his t-shirt and wrapping it around my shoulder to slow the bleeding. "Damn Prez, Moon's gonna fucking kill me."

I smirked at his absurd concern that had the distinction of being true. "Not until she's sure I'll live," I grunted out and turned my attention back to Guapo. With Carlito dead he would now be the head of the Salinas Cartel. His whole family had died protecting the organization and I wasn't naïve enough to think that didn't mean something to a guy like him. It did.

He turned to me, holding the arm where Carlito's bullet had grazed him. The guy really was a lousy fucking shot. "Thank you."

I grinned grimly at his words. "Not a problem. We good?"

Guapo turned back to me. "Yes. We're good. I hope to never see you again."

"Good luck."

Guapo turned his back to me, his business with the Reckless Bastards complete and I knew he had a very big mess to clean up.

HOLIDAY HAVOC

I turned my attention to my own men who were hurt and bloodied, exhausted but alive, and nodded. "Let's go home boys."

Chapter Thirty-Four - Stitch

"Merry Christmas motherfuckers! We made it through another fucking year, can you guys believe it?" I sure as fuck couldn't believe it. No matter how happy I was that the shit I'd stepped in had ended with more than a few non-fatal wounds, it was still unbelievable that we all sat around the table, our ladies at our sides.

Jag grinned the widest, both arms wrapped tight around Vivi. "I believe it. We got the best damn club in the world!" He raised his glass high in the air and waited until we all did the same, beers, wine glasses, shot glasses and cups all went into the air. "To Cross, for leading us through another battle and gettin' us home for Christmas."

"A-fucking-men!" Savior stood and pounded on the table, a gesture sure to rile up all the men. "Drink up, Cross. We gotta get you primed for a world class bachelor party!"

Moon lifted a hand in the air with a smile. "Hold on. Not until after he's off the pain meds." Her eyes went all soft when she looked at Cross, cupping his face and kissing the hell out of him. "He's been banged up enough." Moon had proved me wrong and hadn't threatened to kill anyone. Instead, she'd hugged each of us, kissing both cheeks, for bringing her man back alive.

"Lucky bastard," I told Cross with a wry grin. "That bum shoulder means she does all the work." Marisol smacked my chest at the crude comment, but the slight blush staining her cheeks made me grin. "What? You know it's true."

Marisol rolled her eyes and leaned into me in that way a woman does when she knows she's safe with her man. There were still times when that sadness would get to her and she'd get that blank, terrified look in her eyes but each time it happened it lasted for shorter and shorter periods of time. She still hadn't told me exactly what Carlito and Guapo had done to her but I knew she would.

In time.

"Everyone loves a woman on top," Savior said and pulled Mandy close, smacking a loud kiss right on her red painted lips. "But in all seriousness," he said, voice now stone cold sober as he stood and pulled a bottle of Patron from underneath the table. "We can't celebrate Christmas and not mention our girl who isn't here. Kat. She may be gone but she will never be forgotten."

A chorus of agreement rang out around the table as everyone took a swig of tequila and passed the bottle around. "None for me," Moon said as Cross handed her the heavy bottle. "Booze is a big no-no when you've got a bun in the oven."

Everyone fell silent and all of our gazes landed on Cross, who'd lost his first wife and baby in one fell swoop thanks to that rotten bitch, cancer. He'd been living half a life when I'd met him, fully dedicated to nothing but the club. No women. No fucking. No fun. Now though, since meeting Moon, he was a whole new man. A whole man, period. "You're pregnant?" The question came out quiet, damn near a whisper.

"Yes! *We're* pregnant." She took one of Cross' hands and laid it on her belly with a watery smile. "We're having a baby."

Cross shot out of his seat with a wide and still growing grin. "Holy shit, my junk still works!" He scooped Moon out of her seat and spun her around. "I love you so much, babe."

"I guess that means he's happy about it," Vivi said sarcastically, making the rest of us laugh. "Congratulations, Moon. You're one of those rare women who was born to be a mom."

"Thank you, Vivi."

Jana and Teddy were on their feet and rushing around the table to wrap Moon up in a hug, doing that screechy happy thing that girls did when they were happy or excited, leaving Max and Golden Boy to grab the chairs before they tipped over. "We're going to have another baby shower!" Teddy clapped her hands excitedly, always up to plan any event, big or small.

Moon hugged them both back the way she hugged everyone, with her whole body and full of love. "Let's wait until I'm showing at least, okay?"

"Yeah Teddy, settle down," Jana grinned. "We have more important things to talk about, like the nursery theme."

Cross groaned and slid between Moon and the women. "Let us enjoy this moment before the craziness starts, yeah? Max, Golden Boy, get your baby mamas." Cross laughed at their put out expressions and dipped Moon for a long, hot kiss.

"So," Vivi said when a silence fell around the table. "Jag and I are getting married. Tonight. In Vegas." With a satisfied smile at having shocked us all, she looked around the table. "Everyone is invited but if you don't show up, we'll totally understand."

Teddy slammed her hands on the table angrily. "You're getting married on Christmas Day and you didn't ask me to plan it?" She shot Vivi a fiery glare.

Vivi only shrugged, unphased by Teddy's emotions. "You can plan a reception or something if you want, but I'm not waiting another second to marry this man." With a soft, hazy expression she turned to Jag and smiled before leaning over for a gentle kiss.

"Before the night is over, you'll be mine babe. All mine." And then Jag kissed her and it was so long and hot, so fucking inappropriate, I gripped Marisol's thigh and slid my hand up. That shit was hot.

As fuck.

Cross looked at Moon and smiled a big shit-eating grin. Then to Jag. "We'll be there, man."

"Damn right we will," Moon said with finality. "And you'll all be there on New Year's Day, when Cross and I exchange vows. Right?"

The table fell quiet in shock. "Right," Cross added with a bit more bass in his voice.

"Damn straight," Savior said with a loud whoop.

"Fuck yeah," Jag said with a wide grin, standing to go get more booze.

"Don't worry Teddy," Mandy piped in with a tipsy lean against Savior. "I'm a busy chef and entrepreneur, I'm happy to have you plan our wedding."

Savior frowned. "So you want a big wedding?"

She tossed her blonde head back and laughed. "Babe you have a giant family," she gestured around the table where the entire club sat with their women while the kids all played with their gifts, supervised by a few of the Reckless Bitches. "Or hadn't you noticed?"

Savior smiled in concession to her point and pulled her closer. "Whatever you want, babe." She beamed up at him like he was her own personal hero and ever since Marisol, I knew just how damn powerful that shit felt.

"Damn, everyone is getting married and having babies," Gunnar grumbled. "Feels more like a daycare than a goddamn motorcycle club."

"Don't worry Gunny," Peaches taunted with the dreaded nickname he only allowed Maisie to use but she had somehow taken it for herself as well. "One of these days you'll meet a lady ogre who doesn't mind your shitty, grumpy pants personality and will only care about your fine packaging." Peaches gestured at his body and laughed at her own joke but everyone joined in until Gunnar sent a death glare across the table.

None of us stopped laughing. We were feeling too damn good to stop. Even if it pissed off Gunnar.

He wasn't pissed at all, leaning forward into Peaches' personal space. "You think I'm hot," he said, a rare smile aimed at someone other than Maisie making an appearance. "I knew you fucking wanted me."

"Oh, I want you," she purred. "I want to strip you down, tie you up and beat some manners into you." Her shrug was deceptively casual. "If I could muzzle you, I might take you to bed for real."

Gunnar leaned over and whispered something in Peaches' ear and it must have been filthy because a light flush stained her honey colored skin and her eyes went a little gooey. She was turned on. "We'll see about that muzzle then," he said, his smile a dark promise.

"With all this good news, I'm feeling like a left out old lady," Jana grumbled with a good natured smile. "I never would have thought when I met this big ole biker, that I'd gain this amazing, crazy family. A bunch of rough and tumble motherfuckers who were desperately in need of a woman's touch." She paused a second, her face a light shade of pink. "You guys gave me the confidence to live a full and proud life and I love you all for it. Merry Christmas."

Teddy stood beside her and wrapped an arm around Jana, kissing her cheek. "Yeah, what she said." She waved away our laughter and smiled at each one of us around the table, her eyes wet. "Seriously, even though you unleashed a stalker on me, it brought me Tate and I wouldn't change a thing if it meant I didn't get to have my golden haired cowboy at my side. You Reckless Bastards are the toughest sons of bitches I know, well, aside from Jana, and you are my tribe."

"As much as I appreciate all the girly emotions and shit, if my girl has any more tequila, I won't get any Christmas love tonight and I plan on getting some and getting it good. And all night long," I told them all and stood, grabbing Marisol's hand until she was flush against my chest.

"Ho! Ho! Ho! Merry Mayhem Christmas to all you motherfuckers, and a good *fucking* night."

Epilogue - Max

"Ugh babe, I'm stuffed." I patted my belly after demolishing another round of leftovers and kicked my feet up on the coffee table.

"Maybe one of these Christmases we'll learn not to eat so much." Jana stood in the doorway with one hand on her hip and a playful smile brightening up her face. "I thought you were saving some of those leftovers for me?"

"I did. Plenty of them, actually." She deserved it after slaving away in a hot kitchen for days, cooking enough food for feed the army of Reckless Bastards and their loved ones. And I'd convinced Mandy to give us double the amount and she was happy to, something about being able to fit into a damn wedding dress. "I only killed off three slices of pecan pie."

Jana grinned as she closed the distance between us and climbed up on my lap. "Does that mean I get all the chocolate mousse cake to myself?" She nibbled on my ear as she posed the question, knowing exactly how weak I was when it came to her.

"Keep doing that and you can have whatever you like, sexy lady." Her husky laugh sounded in my ear, her big, soft tits pressed against me and my body started to wake up, food coma be damned.

"I already got everything a girl could possibly want, except maybe a smaller ass."

I rolled my eyes at her complaint, but it gave me a chance to tell her about her fine ass. "I love your ass just the way it is. Don't change a thing," I told her, grabbing both soft ass cheeks in my hand and squeezing to drive the point home. She moaned and I let my lips skitter up and down her neck for a long moment. "You sure you don't want anything else?"

"Like what?" Jana sat back and cupped my cheeks in that soft, loving way she had of reminding me that I meant something to her. "Thanks to you and the club, our babies are all safe and happy. Plus, I've got you, my handsome man."

Yeah, her compliments never failed to get a rise out of me, both literally and figuratively. "Keep going. I like what I'm hearing."

She grinned, and it turned into a laugh. "I'm happy you made it back to me. All in one piece." The fear she'd hidden from me was there in her eyes. "Can you believe it, Max? Two fucked up people like us and we've managed to create this incredible little family." Her eyes went slightly glassy as she took in the images flashing on the digital photo frame I'd given her for Christmas.

Jana loved to take pictures. Especially of me and the kids. It meant I would have to endure all the sneak-attack snapshots and every moment of our lives being captured digitally, but it made her smile and that smile lit up my whole life.

My brow rose at her comment. "Hey, that's my wife you're calling fucked up."

She smiled and laughed just a little, a throaty sound that was somehow sex goddess and girl next door all at once. "You know what I'm saying. It's unlikely that we should have *any* of this, never mind *all* of this. Love and good fortune. And we do. We're making it work, Max. It's like we're blessed. "

"I'm not sure about blessings, but I'd walk through the fires of hell for you. Don't you know you're the best damn thing that's ever happened to me?"

Her pale skin flushed a beautiful shade of pink which was just another reason Jana stole my breath every fucking day, despite her dirty mouth in the bedroom, she still blushed like an innocent girl next door. "Ditto, Max."

She turned in my lap and we sat there for a long time just watching the photos from the day flash before us. "That's my favorite one," she said and pointed to the photo of me, Charlie and Jameson, our gray eyes shining bright for the camera, each of us with a damning chocolate stain at the corners of our mouths. "Those guys right there, they are my whole heart."

"And to think, you wanted nothing to do with me at first." She gasped and shook her head in denial, but I just laughed.

"I liked looking at you, but I was worried. Most men recoil at the sight of my face and I figured you'd be the same."

"Only I wasn't," I said. "From the moment I caught sight of your face, and those big green eyes, I was hooked. And I was a goddamn mess, but you saved me."

"No, I didn't," she insisted. "You saved yourself. And I'm so glad you did because look at us now. We're so blessed. We have a loving home."

"A hot as fuck wife and two strong little boys."

She squirmed on my lap until I groaned and gripped her hips to keep her still. "Hot as fuck?"

"You know you're the hottest thing in all of Nevada, babe. And the whole wide world."

She laughed and poked her soft midsection. "Me? With this baby gut and thunder thighs? You must be in love," she joked and batted her eyelashes prettily.

"You have no idea."

Jana slid off my lap and grinned. "I have some idea, and I have something for you." She disappeared up the stairs, leaving me alone with my thoughts for a moment. I thought about my boys, giggling loudly as they opened up presents. Pint-sized motorcycles, building blocks, trucks and even a miniature ten-gallon cowboy hat for Charlie who believed Lasso to be a real-life cowboy and wanted to be just like him.

My boys were the second and third best thing that had ever happened to me and watching them be normal, healthy, well-adjusted kids made me proud. Hell, made me grateful that a screwed up bastard like me had a hand in them turning out that way. Jana thought I did it, that I was the strong one, but the truth was, Jana was the heart, the soul and the muscle of our family.

"Here we are. Time for grown up gifts." Something altogether different crossed my mind until I looked up, wiggling my eyebrows and saw Jana, weighed down by three large boxes. "Not that kind of grown up, ya big perv!"

"A man can hope, can't he?"

"He doesn't need to hope because I have it on good authority that you're getting lucky tonight." She rolled her eyes and set the boxed on the table in front of me. "Open up and don't be afraid to go crazy like the boys."

I looked up at her and laughed. "Very funny."

"Open them!" She was so excited I found myself tearing at the paper with the snowmen dressed in leather to get to the first box.

"Oh babe, you shouldn't have." It was a brand new leather vest with little mockups of where my patches would go.

"I wasn't sure on protocol for things like that but I saw this vest and I just knew you'd look super hot in it. So go on," she waved her hands at me, "and put it on!"

With a laugh, I did as my woman instructed and slipped on the vest. "Well?"

"Hot as fuck, baby." She licked her lips hungrily and I barely resisted the urge to wrap my lips around her hard nipples peeking through her top. "Next one."

The next gift was for me. In a way. "Jana, I'm afraid this isn't my size."

She laughed and smacked my arm. "It's for me to wear. For you."

"Well this gift is one I can cash in tonight. Right?"

She nodded slowly, her lips in a seductive grin that was fucking irresistible. "We'll see." Green eyes slid to the final and biggest box.

"Damn. You drive a hard bargain, woman." Still I tore into the final box and ripped through the lid and froze. Three little leather jackets were inside, two black and one pink. "Babe? What? Are you...?"

She smiled, her skin flushed a beautiful shade of pink. "No, I'm not pregnant or anything but I think we should keep going until we get a little girl to put that pink jacket on."

I was already sold on that idea. "And if we have two more boys before we have a girl?"

Jana rolled her eyes. "We live a stone's throw from Vegas, I doubt there will be a leather shortage in our future."

I stood and pulled Jana in my arms. "You sure you want that many kids with an old fucker like me?"

She smiled and jumped into my arms. "I want a whole fucking brood with my handsome husband who can sometimes be a little surly, but I love him anyway."

How in the hell a guy like me got so lucky that a beautiful, talented woman and loving mother like Jana fell for me and married me, I'd never know. All I knew was, I'd spend the rest of my life being worthy of her. Of our family, however big it grew. "Good because he loves you more than anything."

"Yeah? Wait until he gets a load of me in that leather dress."

Before I could say anything, her lips were on mine, slow and deep they way she always kissed, like every damn time she wasn't just showing me how much she loved me, she was telling me too. With every slide of her tongue I swear I fell deeper in love with this woman. With *my* woman.

"Babe in or out of that dress, more out of than in though, hey!" I laughed when she nipped my ear a bit too hard. "I love you no matter what, that's all I'm trying to say babe."

"Yeah?" Her smile was big, her skin flushed and those big ol' emerald eyes shone with love. More love than I thought I deserved when I met her.

I nodded. "Fuck yeah, and you know what else?"

"What, Max?" The way she held my jaw, gentle and loving with a smile filled with heat.

"I was just thinking, it was so fuckin' hot the way you told me to go out there and kill those motherfuckers, I rode to the desert with a boner." She laughed and tightened her legs around my waist.

"You have one now too. Yay! Merry Christmas to me!" Then she ground against me, put her lips to my throat and her mouth didn't leave my body for the rest of the night.

Other than to refuel with holiday leftovers. "Would you still love me if I told you I didn't know what tasted better, Christmas leftovers or you?"

Jana cocked her eyebrow with a sexy smile on her face. Damn, she was beautiful. "No but I will be mad unless you do some very thorough research and come up with a *satisfying* answer…"

I grinned. This Christmas was unlike any of the others Jana and I had spent together. This time we had two little boys, a bigger family and we'd faced our biggest threat yet and come out on top. "If it's for the sake of research, consider me in babe."

And I spent the rest of the night doing science. Between the gorgeous legs of my beautiful wife.

I was pretty sure in that moment, life for the Reckless Bastard's couldn't get any better.

Merry friggin' Christmas to us!

* * * *

~ THE END ~

Acknowledgements

Thank you so much for making my books a success! I appreciate all of you! Thanks to all of my beta readers, street teamers, ARC readers and Facebook fans. Y'all are THE BEST!

And a huge very special thanks to Jessie! I'm such a *hot mess, but without your keen sense of organization and skills, I'd be a burny fiery inferno of hot mess!! Thank you!

And a very special thanks to my editors (who sometimes have to work all through the night! *See HOT MESS above!) Thank you for making my words make sense.

Copyright © 2018 KB Winters and BookBoyfriends Publishing LLC

KB WINTERS

About The Author

KB Winters is a Wall Street Journal and USA Today Bestselling Author of steamy hot books about Bikers, Billionaires, Bad Boys and Badass Military Men. Just the way you like them. She has an addiction to caffeine, tattoos and hard-bodied alpha males. The men in her books are very sexy, protective and sometimes bossy, her ladies are...well...*bossier*!

Living in sunny Southern California, with her five kids and three fur babies, this embarrassingly hopeless romantic writes every chance she gets!

You can reach me at Facebook.com/kbwintersauthor and at kbwintersauthor@gmail.com

Copyright © 2018 KB Winters and BookBoyfriends Publishing LLC

Printed in Great Britain
by Amazon